P9-DVB-759

The Cathay Stories And Other Fictions

THE CATHAY STORIES AND OTHER FICTIONS

BY

MACDONALD HARRIS

Story Line Press

THIS SERIES IS MADE POSSIBLE BY THE GENEROUS SUPPORT
of the
NICHOLAS ROERICH MUSEUM, NEW YORK

Printed in the United States of America

•

ISBN: 0-934257-13-2 (paper)
0-934257-14-0 (cloth)

•

Published by Story Line Press
A subsidiary of The Reaper, Inc.
325 Ocean View Avenue
Santa Cruz, California 95062

•

Book design and cover by Lysa Howard-McDowell
Cover: Portmerion, Wales
Typesetting by TypaGraphix

•

Library of Congress Cataloging-in-Publication Data 88-60346

ACKNOWLEDGEMENTS

In preparing this book I have been grateful for the advice and help of a number of people, especially Bob Miles, Robert Peters, Barbara Haas, Mary Evans of Virginia Barber Literary Agency, and my editor Robert McDowell.

PERMISSIONS

"The Dog Mafia" and "Dr. Pettigot's Face" have previously appeared in *The Iowa Review*, and "The Photograph" has appeared in *The Redlands Review*. Publication is by permission.

For Patricia Geary

CONTENTS

POLO'S TRIP

His Excellency the Consul General of Venice
Xanadu
Celestial Kingdom of Cathay

My dear Mr. Consul General, excuse me if I don't know how to address you properly, I hadn't expected to have to write this letter and I don't have the reference materials at hand to verify your correct form of title. You see in me a thing which you probably encounter quite frequently in your profession, a traveler in distress in the country to which you are accredited, and in which a part of your duties is the rendering of assistance and advice to your fellow citizens. I am not even sure where I am, except that it's somewhere on the border, and there is an officer named Mu in charge. Perhaps that information would enable you to check with the authorities and determine the approximate location, at least, of the place from which I am writing. I doubt if it is important enough to have a name.

What am I doing here anyhow? You may well ask that, and it is to explain this that I am engaged, under the most difficult circumstances imaginable and lacking even the most rudimentary of materials, in inditing this communication to you, whoever you are and *if indeed you exist* —this is what I am beginning to doubt.

I began this trip on the fifteenth of May, although I am not sure how long ago that was, because I've lost track of the calendar. Anyhow, as I recollect (curse this pen, it seems to be a buzzard feather), my Uncle Maffeo offered to drive me to the Milan airport, since there was no direct flight from Venice to Karachi. This was a trip of only an hour or so on the autostrada, and he spent most of it trying to persuade me not to go.

"It's a folly," he said. "Why?"

"Well, I'm young. It's the time for follies."

He said, "I don't know what's got into you. You have your degree in physics from Padua, a brilliant career lies ahead of you, there is your Uncle Zeno in America who is ready to offer you a position in his company, you are engaged to a beautiful girl whose father also happens to be a millionaire."

"I wouldn't say Cristina is beautiful. She's a nice enough girl."

He said, "She's beautiful. She has a beautiful soul. A promising future—your family willing and ready to help—we've given you a sports car, a villa in Sardinia, vacations at a ski resort . . . I don't understand young people any more. They don't seem to want to get ahead in the world as we did. You could apply for a university chair, do research, go into administration, whatever you wanted.

"I'm doing exactly what I want."

He said, "You're a good-looking young rascal and you have winning ways. You're successful with women—don't raise your hand in protest—I have my sources. A few judicious caresses to the wives of influential men . . . "

"What about Cristina, that beautiful soul?"

"Cristina," he said, "could go and live in America with you. Zeno's factory is in Schenectady, which is a beautiful city on the Hudson River, filled with magnificent works of art, and with an excellent chamber orchestra."

Maffeo knew nothing whatsoever about America and had no idea where Schenectady was. I was impressed, however, that he managed to pronounce the word. I'm the linguist of the family; languages come easily to me and I possess eight or ten of them. He knows only Italian and Venetian, and prefers to speak the latter when he is among friends.

"Perhaps I'll come back, at some later time, and marry Cristina after all. If she really loves me she'll wait."

He said, "To throw away such advantages! The influence of your relatives! And the finest education in the world!"

I sighed. He exaggerated so terribly that it was hard to talk to him. "Padua is an excellent university, but probably the best ones in the world for physics are Cambridge and M.I.T."

He said, "You could do postgraduate work! We could send you to England! That's not the end of the world. Or to M.I.T.! It's located in Boston, a beautiful city on the Mississippi River, full of magnificent art treasures, with an excellent symphony orchestra."

"Actually it's in Cambridge."

"No, Cambridge University is in Cambridge. M.I.T. is in Boston."

"Cambridge, Massachusetts. It's in America."

"Cambridge, Massachusetts. A beautiful city. They say the women there are spectacular. You could do your research in the Smithsonian."

And so on. "Thank you for driving me, Uncle. I wouldn't have wanted to leave my Alfa here in Milan. I may be gone for some time."

We had, in fact, arrived at the airport. I glanced at my watch. It was an excellent instrument, a Seiko. I had only five minutes or so. "Hurry, Uncle." I leapt out in front of the terminal, grabbing my old leather suitcase from the back seat.

"Is that all the baggage you have, to go to the end of the world? One last time, Polo. Think what you are doing. A magnificent career—a life with Cristina—your whole future lies ahead of you. And besides," he shouted after me, "it's too late for you to make this trip now."

"Too late?" In my haste I scarcely paid attention to what he was saying.

"Yes, if you wanted to go you should have started a long time ago."

"Ciao, Uncle."

In Karachi there was an interesting contretemps with the baggage. I was waiting at the carrousel along with everybody else—for some reason my bag is always the last to come off, whether I board the plane early or late. Then I caught sight of it, or thought I did, bumping along behind a blue streamlined Samsonite and an overstuffed backpack. It was a large horsehide affair that had belonged to my father, covered with scratches, a dark brown in some places and black in others. I usually tied a stout cord around it, since the locks at the top were unreliable, and the first thing I noticed was that this cord was missing. However, I thought nothing about it. The cord could easily have come off while the suitcase was being flung around with the traditional violence by the baggage-handlers. I pressed my way forward through the throng, pushing people aside and provoking indignant murmurs, and was about to set my hand on it when it was abruptly taken away by a man I hadn't noticed before, a short distance away on the upstream side, so to speak, of the direction the carrousel was moving. He was a short bald man of Levantine complexion, wearing a dirty raincoat and the shifty expression of a criminal or a secret masturbator. This person, who seemed to possess considerable muscular strength, jerked the bag off the moving belt before I could grasp what had happened, and was making off with it in a kind of rapid slouch. I chased him and grabbed the handle of the suitcase, with his greasy hand crushed against my own. When he looked around at me his furtive expression turned to a snarl of hostility, although he said nothing. Perhaps he didn't speak any of the usual civilized tongues. There was a brief tussle that left me panting. He bared his teeth at me, and I pulled with all my strength. Then, looking around for someone to help, I caught a glimpse of another brownish horsehide suitcase coming around the carrousel, identical to my own; in fact it probably was my own. I let go of the suitcase I was holding. "Excuse me," I said. "Pardon. Scusate. Entschuldigung. Perdon. Förlåt."

Whether or not he knew any of these languages, he didn't hear me. He was already out the door of the terminal. I hurried back and waited for the other bag to come around—it had already disappeared around the merry-go-round by this time. I retrieved it without any difficulty; the crowd around the carrousel had almost dispersed. There was no cord around this one either but that meant nothing. It was identical to my own; I thought I could even recognize the same scratches. It had been battered a little more during the flight so that one corner was dented in, and attached to the handle was a plastic tag with the inscription "H. Karagian."

H. Karagian was probably clear out of the airport in his taxi by this time. I considered going to the police, or complaining to the baggage department of the airline, but a curious mood of insouciance had come over me since I had begun this trip. I reasoned: there was nothing in particular of value in my own suitcase except my travelers checks, and according to all the advertisements they were replaceable. Whatever H. Karagian had in his suitcase, it was quite likely as valuable as what I had in my own. I couldn't see myself wearing his clothes, but I took a certain amusement in imagining him in my tennis shorts, or in the oriental kimono I sometimes fancied for boudoir scenes, just for a joke. Let H. Karagian have it! Whatever *he* had, it was mine now. I could hardly wait to get to the hotel to see what treasures had come into my possession.

There was one thing about H. Karagian's suitcase, it was heavy as hell. It weighed twice as much as my own. I could barely get it into the taxi, and when I got to the hotel I had to pay fifty rupees (I think they were called) to the doorman before he would deign to struggle with it into the foyer. I went up with it in the elevator, and once I was alone in my room with it and the door locked, I gazed at it with a certain curiosity. It was certainly not my own; for one thing the locks were in better condition. In fact they were locked and I couldn't get them open. Searching about in the room, I found a tool intended for opening soft-drink cans, and with this I was able to prize at the locks enough so that they popped open. I wouldn't be able to shut them again, of course, but I could probably borrow a length of stout cord from the hotel management.

I soon found out why the infernal thing was so heavy. For the most part it was filled with small neatly-tied bags of coins. Krugerrands—I untied a bag and took one out to look at it. It was brand-new and shiny. There was some kind of a leaping animal on it in bas-relief, perhaps a springbok, and below it the legend "Fyngoud—1 oz—Fine Gold." Without counting, I judged that there were a hundred or so coins in each bag, and there were at least a dozen bags. I put the coin I had taken out into my pocket and tied the canvas bag up again.

For the rest, H. Karagian's possessions seemed to consist mainly of disguises. There was the uniform of a colonel of the Indian army—I couldn't tell which regiment, but the band on the peaked cap was crimson. A baton went with this; it was a smart turn-out. There were a number of others. A Bedouin burnoose, with the usual red-and-white checked shawl to tie around your face in sandstorms. A pair of oil-stained mechanic's overalls with "Air Pakistan" over the pocket—this must have been useful to get into airports without going through the security check. The plaid polyester pants, maroon blazer, and porkpie hat of an American tourist. There was what appeared to be a camera to go along with this, but it was only an empty case with a sandwich in it. The white ihraam of a Mecca pilgrim; no Moslem policeman would stop a haji, even one carrying a heavy suitcase. A khaki safari outfit, including a cork-lined topi and a shooting-jacket with loops for bullets. An Iranian chadar, the black garmet that covers women from head to foot and allows only their eyes to be seen. The last costume I couldn't quite figure out; it was a saffron-colored affair of flimsy silk, and it may have been something worn by Buddhist monks or by dancing-girls in Beirut. There were also twenty-three pairs of sunglasses of all types and colors—I counted them.

I put all of this back in the suitcase. Lacking a stout cord, I ran the Indian colonel's belt around the suitcase and cinched it tight. It was a very versatile belt. It was at least a meter and a half long and punched full of holes at even intervals, so that it would fit anybody from a ninety-pound boy to H. Karagian himself, who, from the fragmentary glimpse I had caught of him, was rather portly.

It goes without saying that I was pleased with this sleight-of-hand that fate had played me with the suitcases, and for more reasons than the obvious ones. With a malicious satisfaction I imagined H. Karagian at the wicket of a bank with my travelers checks, trying to persuade someone that his name was Polo. I had already derived my due pleasure from the thought of him in the kimono or the tennis shorts. He couldn't use a silver-backed hairbrush since he was bald. As for my high-quality German condoms, he could do as he pleased with them. Considering how repulsive he was, I doubted that he could persuade anybody to let him insert one into her, and you didn't need them for masturbation. Of course, he could do all kinds of things with his Krugerrands. But he didn't have his Krugerrands anymore.

I went down to a sumptuous dinner of roast lamb, curry, and Algerian wine. I wasn't concerned about leaving the suitcase unguarded in the hotel room. I felt that a treasure that had come into my possession so effortlessly must be charmed, and anyone who tampered with it would be struck dead by fate, or enchanted blind by angels and carried off, perhaps, to a remote corner of Minnesota. Besides I still had a single Krugerrand in my pocket. This was worth more, probably, than my own suitcase and everything in it. Even if the suitcase were stolen now I would still come out ahead.

The next morning there was a little difficulty with financial calculations when I went to pay the bill. With dinner and breakfast it came to about three hundred rupees.

I asked the clerk, "How many rupees for a Krugerrand?"

"I have no idea. What is a Krugerrand?"

"Go and ask somebody," I told him. "Hurry up, I haven't much time."

He came back and reported that eight rupees was one dollar, and that a Krugerrand was six hundred dollars. He actually got out an abacus. I had thought that everyone had a hand calculator in this day and age, but I was getting into a more backward part of the world. Therefore a Krugerrand was forty-eight hundred rupees.

I told him to keep the change. He showed no surprise at this. Perhaps he believed I was making a mistake in my calculations but thought it best to say nothing, or perhaps he simply thought that all foreigners are a little crazy. All foreigners *are* a little crazy, in my experience. That is, they don't think as we do. I am aware of that as a Venetian. Even the Milanese are a little crazy, and Romans more so. As for Americans, or Argentinians . . .

On the drive to the airport, I opened the suitcase and got out another Krugerrand to give to the taxi driver.

The airline equipment deteriorated sharply after I left Karachi and headed on to the east, and so, in my opinion, did the personnel. The line that I had booked on—I had no choice, since it was the only one that had service to the place I wanted to get to—was called the East and North Orient Air Way. It may be that the lack of a plural came from an imperfect grasp of English, or it may have indicated that they had only one plane. If so, I flew on it—an antique DC-3 that bore traces of the paint of a half-dozen other airlines on it, and at the bottom some khaki that seemed to indicate that it had originally served a military purpose of some sort. The engines leaked oil, the cabin was not pressurized, and the doors would not shut properly. They whistled in flight like banshees, the pitch of their note providing an approximate air-speed indicator for the hapless passengers. Shortly after we took off, the single flight attendant, a strand of hair already working loose at her temple, took the microphone. "I am Fatima and I will be assisting you on this flight. There will be a simple lunch in an hour. Please do not chew betel or smoke cigars. Alcohol may not be served while passing over Benares, Oman, or Mount Athos. For more technical questions, such as the altitude of our twin-engine Douglas Cloudliner or its speed forward through the air, please address yourself to Captain Saĭd himself, should he be passing through on his way to the convenience, which is in the rear of the plane." Already tired, tucking the hair into place, she hung up the microphone without any expression on her face. There didn't seem to be any copilot. She went up into the cockpit and sat down next to the pilot. We could hear them up there, eating loukoumi and talking loudly over the noise of the engines.

In this interesting museum piece we flew all day to the east, landing now and then at constantly more remote and primitive airports to let off a passenger or two: a Greek priest in Lahore, a pregnant woman in Amritsar, a German commercial traveler and a pair of Jainist pilgrims in Thok Jalung. The last stop was at Uqbar, where the Douglas disgorged a pair of American lovebirds named Giles and Linda who were going to spend their honeymoon working in the Peace Corps. They went happily off toward the only building in sight, a kind of military barracks at the edge of the runway. I hoped they hadn't been brought to the wrong place by mistake. They disappeared into the barracks and that was the end of them. The only Uqbari in sight were a number of soldiers standing about with antiquated rifles. The fuel tanks of the plane were almost empty, and I was recruited to help Captain Saĭd bargain for more, partly in Uqbari from a dictionary he had in the cockpit and partly in a kind of international patois. ("Benzina. Prix? Dollars. What octane?"). The fuel, when it was brought up in a lot of rusty iron barrels, was really nasty-looking stuff. But when it was in the tanks the two engines started, at least. An officer waved the plane on its way with a kind of disdainful gesture. As it began to move a soldier sprang forward and threatened the rolling tire with his bayonet. Captain Saïd pushed the throttles forward all the way; there was a roar and a blast of dust and the soldier retreated. We were in the air. The bad fuel sputtered but we slowly gained altitude, probably enough to clear the snowy peaks to the east.

"Would you care for a piece of loukoumi?" Fatima asked me, offering the box.

I was the only passenger left now. This made Captain Saïd quite out of sorts. But he had to deliver me where I was going; I had paid my fare and the destination was clearly indicated on the ticket. Over the roar of the engines I could hear Fatima and Captain Saïd discussing the incompetency of the Karachi ticket agent, who was a nephew of the director of the company. "Five hundred miles for one passenger," I heard him yelling at her. "And this goat-pasture where he wants to land is even worse than the field at Uqbar."

It really wasn't so bad. It was a dirt airstrip, but it was fairly straight and there were only a few bumps on it. And once we were on the ground and came to a stop we weren't bothered at all by any soldiers waving bayonets. In fact not a living soul came out to meet the plane. Captain Saïd left the engines grumbling and the propellors whirling like big pinwheels while Fatima unfastened a door in the bowels of the plane and extricated my suitcase. "A heavy bugger," she grunted, sweating.

As far as I would tell the plane had simply stopped at the end of the runway. A dry wind blew a veil of shimmering dust across the dirt under our feet. There were some fecaloid-shaped mountains in the distance.

"Where's the terminal?"

Without speaking she pointed behind her back to a large tin-roofed building, constructed partly of wood and partly of the native stone that was rampant in that part of the world; there were several chunks of it in fact lying on the landing strip.

"That looks to me like a warehouse."

"Well, if you can find a better terminal you're welcome to it."

She got back into the plane, pulled up the ladder, and shut the door. Even before it was completely latched Captain Saïd pushed open his throttles and kicked around the rudder. Like the soldier with his bayonet, I found myself blasted out of the path of the already rolling plane by the hurricane from the propellors. Dust and grit flew into my eyes. I'll never travel on that line again, I told myself. Of course, no other airline came to this part of the world, and even this one didn't.

When the plane was gone, racing dustily away down the landing strip, I was able to get a clearer picture of the place I had arrived at. In addition to the terminal or warehouse, there was a kind of bungalow on a low bluff overlooking the airstrip, and a short distance from it what appeared to be an outdoor privy. A little farther along there was a small hut, constructed entirely of stone, with a timber door and iron bars over the windows. That was all. All four buildings had the same sort of tin roof, so-called, although I as a scientist knew that they were actually corrugated iron, now converted through the passage of time very largely into ferric oxide. The topography was typical of the high-desert country found in many places of the world. The roughly oblong valley was ringed with mountains. For flora, some dry brush, and for fauna a brown lizard doing push-ups on one of the chunks of rock lying around on the moonscape. "They say the Lion and the Lizard keep, the Courts where Jamshyd gloried and drank deep." No sign of lions. I picked up my suitcase and began struggling with it toward the so-called terminal, which was farther away than it looked.

According to a crudely painted sign on the building the place was called Kut, or Tuk, depending on whether you read the local language from left to right or from right to left. The building *was* a warehouse. It was windowless, with a single enormous door, and a kind of loading dock in front of it. There was no one to stop me at the door and I entered. Inside it was suddenly cool. It was really only hot in the sun, and once I was out of it the desert air quickly dried my perspiration. The building was full of bales of what appeared to be the hides of some small animal. Perhaps Captain Saĭd was right and the place was a goat pasture. More probably, however, the hides were those of some indigenous feral creature like the gazelle. I didn't know what anyone would want them for.

There appeared a bandit; I can only describe him as such. In addition to a pair of ferocious mustaches he wore a collarless smock, a dirty skirt, and a pair of sheepherder's boots. A revolver in an ancient holster hung from his belt, and he had a bandoleer of bullets over his shoulder.

He studied me. "Onglash," he accused.

"No, Venashian."

"Ah. Piacha Shan Marco. Gondolash."

"That's it." Evidently someone around here subscribed to the *National Geographic*. I was soon to find out who it was.

"You watchman?"

"Ga."

"What you name?"

"Bahram."

"Where hotel?"

He pointed to the bungalow on the low bluff. We were still inside the warehouse, but there was nothing else to point at in the valley, and I knew that this was what he was indicating.

"Carry my suitcase there?"

"Rupee."

"How about a Krugerrand?"

"Okay."

I had noticed before that this word was becoming international. The phenomenon was called cultural rape. If it extended far enough, there might even be a Coca-Cola around.

"Are you sure I can stay at the hotel?"

"Ga."

When we got to the so-called hotel, the bungalow, we found it in charge of an Englishman named Gresseth-Jones, barefoot, in a madras shirt and dirty khaki pants. He greeted me warmly; he was friendly and hospitable, even jovial, not to say drunk. He offered me a brandy in a not very clean tumbler, filling up his own again at the same time. No chance of a Coca-Cola. "It's imported," he told me, lifting the glass up and sipping it with savor. This was evidently his idea of a joke. As near as I could tell from examining the bottle, it was made in Morocco.

After we had finished our drink (two or three for him) he showed me around the place. There was a kitchen in which you could build a bonfire inside a brick box. The drawing room, as he called it, had nothing in it but some worn carpets, an antique cheval-glass, a pile of torn *National Geographics*, and a broken-open case of the Moroccan brandy. His own bedroom was provided with a colonial bedstead of the Victorian epoch, complete with mosquito net. The rifle hanging on the wall was to match; it was a Martini-Henry. As for me, he invited me to sleep on the veranda in a hammock. He showed me this contrivance; it resembled a shawl sewn onto two sticks. The well was in the courtyard. As for the other sanitary conveniences, I had already glimpsed them from the landing strip.

"Are there any women around?"

"No, no women can be induced to live in the place. We do have some sucking-boys if that interests you."

It didn't. "What's that other building over there?" I pointed to the small stone hut with the barred windows.

"Ah that. The calaboose. Durance Vile, you know."

"So you have crime?"

"Not crime exactly," he said vaguely. "Sometimes a chap will get intractable and we have to put him in there for a few days to reflect on his sins. It's the sun drives them mad, you know. When one of them goes amok, Bahram can round him up with no trouble. He and I are the only ones in the place who have guns."

"I thought Bahram was the watchman."

"He's also the police force. And the army."

I gathered that he, that is Gresseth-Jones, was the manager and general king of the place, more or less in the manner of Mr. Kurtz at the Inner Station. He didn't have a row of skulls on posts, but he did have a warehouse full of hides which seemed to me vaguely sinister. His own explanation of them was unsatisfactory, although entertaining. According to him, they were the hides of the foetuses of wild asses, highly valued in parts of the world for shoes, gloves, and other fine maroquinerie. Anybody who had a gun (that confined it pretty much to him and Bahram) shot wild asses from horseback; it was the only sport in the place. For the most part the corpses were left to desiccate in the sun. In case the victim was pregnant, the foetus was removed and its hide added to those in the bales. Unfortunately, the animal in question, *Asinus asiaticus goldsmithi*, was an endangered species and there was an international embargo against exporting their skins. That was why there were so many in the warehouse. They had been accumulating there for eighty years.

"Then how do you live?"

"By sucking our teeth. There are some nomads around," he said, "who bring in a little booty now and then."

I stayed with Gresseth Jones for several days, waiting for "transport" as he called it. If there was to be such, only he could arrange it. Or so he gave me to understand. However he was a cheerful enough fellow and entertaining in his way. While I was waiting (and at this point, of course, I had no idea whether my sojourn in Kut or Tuk would amount to three days or three months) he regaled me with a constant flow of disconnected chatter, mostly about himself. I never did succeed in finding out exactly who he was. He told many stories about himself and other things, most of them invented on the spot as far as I could tell: that he was the son of an earl, that he was a multiple murderer sought in seven European countries, that the sister of the Queen of England had once been his mistress, that the mountains thereabouts were full of wild dogs who had once eaten a whole party of archeologists, that it is possible to live on gin since the juniper-oil with which it is flavored contains all vitamins, and so on. As near as I could gather he was a photographer by profession, although all he had to show in evidence of this was a Japanese wide-angle lens, broken, that corresponded to no camera in his possession. There was even some doubt about his name. He called himself sometimes Gresseth-Jones, sometimes Jones-Gresseth, or occasionally the one without the other or vice versa. Like many egomaniacs he frequently spoke of himself in the third person: "They've tried a thousand tricks to catch old Jones but they haven't succeeded yet." It was patently impossible for all of this to be true, and he even confessed some of his fictions to me. Suggesting to me once that his real name was Thistlethwaite, he immediately after admitted that this was only a blague for the purpose of confounding the local linguists (perhaps Bahram was one of them) who claimed or believed that they knew some English; he took a joy in seeing them tongue-tied for hours on end, locked in struggle with the labio-dental sibillants.

"About my transport," I pressed him now and then.

"Ah yes. Well, it's difficult. Everything is difficult in this part of the world. Patience is needed. I've forgotten where it was you said you wanted to go." This was very likely, since he sometimes forgot his own name, and simple facts such as whether we had already had our lunch or not or whether Islam was monotheistic.

"Well, to the east," I said, not wishing to give too much away to him. "Let's call it, in a general way, the Orient."

"It's no good trying to be secretive with me, old man. I know very well what you're talking about." He took a great swallow of the brandy in his glass and then stared at me fixedly.

"Have you been there?"

"Well, I won't say I have and I won't say I haven't."

"What *will* you say?"

"That a chap should think twice about it."

"I've already thought twice about it."

"Perhaps you should think three times. Facilis descensus Averni, you know."

"Ah, you're a Latinist."

"I have the usual public school education. Easy is the descent into Hell, but to return, to come back, that is more difficult. *Aeneid VI*, line 126 and eff eff."

"Cathay then is Hell, according to you?"

"Avernus, Virgil says. It's not quite the same thing."

"Yes, but we're talking about Cathay."

"Ah, are we? I thought we were talking about Virgil. A magnificent poet. I know his Fourth Eclogue by heart. Or I did once."

"Whatever we're talking about, I'm sure it's not the Fourth Eclogue. What exactly is the analogy between the problem of going to Cathay and the passage you cite from the Sixth Book of the *Aeneid*?"

"Analogy? Ah well. You'll find out soon enough. They hate our guts there, you know."

"I'm familiar with xenophobia. I've already been to Uqbar and came away from it unscathed."

"Ah, have you," he said, showing interest. "You must tell me about it sometime."

"I will, but right now we're talking about Cathay. Do you mean they will do me some harm there?"

"Harm, harm. What's harm. You won't come away, that's all."

"Have you been there or not?" I asked him flatly.

He stood up and slammed down his glass. "Been there! Been there!" he shouted, stalking around the room. "How could I have been there! How could I have not been there! Let me tell you, old chap, once you've been there, you don't ask yourself whether you've been there or not. It's a question qui ne se pose pas. Or ne suppose pas, I'm not sure which. One thing I can tell you with assurance, and that is that you can go there as easy as say Snap Johnny but you won't come back alive."

"Are you alive?"

"That's a question I often ask myself. Que je me pose

souvent. Que je suppose souvent."

At this point he poured himself some more brandy. I began to suspect that I was dealing with a dangerous lunatic. The thing was to stop pressing him with questions about Cathay and concentrate on the problem of transport.

"Is there air service?"

"It's easy to see you know nothing about the place," he said contemptuously.

In this way I spent a number of days in this God-forsaken place, constantly pestering Gresseth-Jones with questions about transport and picking up whatever morsels of information I could about Cathay from his occasional hints and innuendoes, and from the pile of magazines in the bungalow. Except for reading the *National Geographic* there wasn't much to do in Tuk or Kut. I could see how it had driven Gresseth-Jones batty. The meals were served on time, in pukka sahib tradition. We had Turkish coffee for breakfast, and for lunch and dinner a stew made of meat which I hoped was goat, but suspected was that of the wild asses whose progeny was never to be made into gloves. Perhaps it was the foetus-meat itself; it was certainly tender enough. At tea-time, brandy; but this made it no different from any other time of the day. Once in a while when Gresseth-Jones was in the privy (he was suffering from constipation and spent several hours each day in there) I set off to explore the place, as well as I could on foot. I had already seen the airstrip and the warehouse, Gresseth-Jones was in the privy, and the only other improvement in sight was the jail or calaboose. When I approached this I found it was not really such a ramshackle affair as it appeared from a distance; it was built of native stone but the stones were firmly cemented in place, and the door was made of timbers a foot thick. Applying my face to one of the two barred windows, I stared into the darkness inside. After a while I made out several pairs of floating, egg-like, luminescent objects, crossing each other, rising and falling, and ceasing in their aimless drifting after a while to stop and stare back at me.

"Salaam," I said experimentally.

"Onglash?"

I didn't really think it was Bahram in there. Perhaps it was the stock question to apply to strangers in these parts. In any case, the conversation didn't seem a promising one and I turned away to continue along a path I now perceived leading on across the bluff, little more than a scratch in the red sand. Following this, I came after five minutes or so on an improvement I hadn't noticed before. Two rude wooden crosses were stuck into a mound of earth a little redder than the sand around it. On one of them the word "Carlier" had been scratched with a nail, and on the other "Kayerts." The mound had evidently been there a long time; the indigenous desert-brush was already growing over it about as thickly as it did on the terrain around.

Beyond the cemetery, if this was what it was, there didn't seem to be anything more to see. The red valley floor stretched off to the mountains, rising up a little as it approached them. It occurred to me that Gresseth-Jones had spoken of hunting from horseback, but there were no horses in sight, or no stable either. Perhaps the horses were kept in the mountains, along with the wild dogs who ate archeologists. If this were so, did Gresseth-Jones first make his way on foot to the mountains, when he wanted to go hunting? He could barely get around the drawing room, and his bottle of brandy wouldn't last to the mountains and back. There were many mysteries. Probably there weren't any wild asses. If not, what had we eaten for lunch?

On the way back to the bungalow I met Gresseth-Jones just coming out of the privy. He seemed quite cheerful. Evidently the visit had been a success.

"Who were Carlier and Kayerts?" I asked him.

"Ah yes. They're characters in Conrad. A story called An Outpost of Progress. It's a riot. Have you read it?"

"You know," I told him, "it's that stew that's causing your trouble. You ought to eat a diet with more bulk."

"There's nothing else to eat around here except this thorny-brush."

"You could try growing some vegetables."

"I detest vegetables, old chap."

As soon as we got back to the bungalow, however, he told me that he had solved my transport problem. Since it had been unsolved only an hour before, the sequence of events suggested that he had talked to somebody in the privy about it, or more probably that he had merely thought out what to do about it while he was in there. He didn't say what the transport would consist of. He did say, however, "You can't wear those clothes, you know."

"I can't?"

"No. You see, westerners have been attacked on the route. We're not popular. After all it's their country, you know."

I wondered if this generality included Kut or Tuk itself, but I didn't pursue the question. "I have some other clothes, as a matter of fact."

"Have you? Well, that's very foresighted of you."

It wasn't that exactly, but the matter was too complicated to explain. "I could disguise myself," I told him, "as several other people. Would you recommend a Bedouin or an Indian colonel?"

"I beg your pardon? Well, we'd better have a look at these things, old man."

I tried several of the costumes on for him, standing in front of the battered old tilting cheval-glass in the drawing room. I myself was attracted to the Indian colonel. The uniform even fitted me to an extent, which seemed to suggest that it could never have fitted H. Karagian. I put on the smart cap with the red band, tipped it a little to one side, and took the baton in my hand.

"You're not the military type, old chap. You'd never fool 'em."

I dismissed the Air Pakistan mechanic's overalls, since there was no air service where I was going. The Bedouin burnoose was very comfortable, I had to admit. It did leave an airy feeling down around one's genitals. It was a pleasant sensation and some interesting theories began to occur to me as to why women wore skirts. Gresseth-Jones had nothing much to say about this except "H'mmm." He seemed thoughtful. It was a possibility.

I took it off and disguised myself as an American tourist, just for fun, even though it was a western costume like my own and so not suitable. Along with the plaid pants, maroon blazer, and porkpie hat was a Hawaiian shirt made in Brooklyn, New York. The shoes were tassel mocassins. I put all this on and hung the camera case around my neck by its strap, discarding the sandwich.

We both looked at the reflection in the mirror.

"Try to get a look of idiotic friendliness on your face."

I tried.

"No, it won't do. You're hopelessly European and cynical."

We both excluded the Iranian chadar. In the end it came down to the burnoose and the safari outfit. The cork-lined topi was a little loose, until I found it was adjustable and tightened the strap that ran around the inside. H. Karagian had a rather large head for so stubby a man.

"It depends in the end, old chap, on whether you want

to blend into the landscape, so to speak, or come out in an aggressive way and dominate things. The bullet loops, don't you see, in the safari jacket. They might be regarded as bellicose by peace-loving natives."

"There are no bullets in them."

"It's a symbolic thing, old man. It's even worse if there are no bullets. If there were bullets in them, it might inspire some respect."

"You could lend me some bullets."

"No I couldn't. On the whole I opt for the burnoose. You see, old chap, there's something you haven't thought of, and that is that a burnoose is a loose sort of garment so that you can carry all sorts of things on you, bullets or whatever, and they won't be seen because they're under the burnoose. From the point of view of sartorial theory, it's at the opposite pole from the safari jacket, which is a way of showing the flag, so to speak, by flaunting your bullets on your chest. It's like gunboat diplomacy."

"You have quite a gift for metaphor."

"I have many gifts, old man, but they're all wasted in this effing arse-hole of the world. Try on the burnoose again."

It was a very efficient garment. The various peoples of the world, I reflected, knew what they were doing when over a long period of time they developed clothing suitable to their climate and topography. The burnoose was white and would shed sunlight, but it was also warm when it was cold. It offered protection from sandstorms. It was hat, coat, and trousers all at once, and it could easily be washed in any random waterhole. It did not require for any purpose the awkward business of taking your pants off, a degrading ceremony found only in western civilizations. There were some sandals that went with it. The red-and-white checked shawl could be used for any number of purposes—wrapped around your head, utilized as a face-towel, or knotted into a bag for carrying medium-sized objects.

"The burnoose," I decided.

"You're doing the right thing, old chap."

"When will I leave?"

"At nightfall. From the warehouse. I'll have to ask you for some money by the way. These chaps won't do anything for nothing."

"You're taking your cut, of course."

"My dear chap."

I opened the suitcase again, untied one of the canvas bags, and spilled a few of the coins out into the palm of my hand.

"Oh my blessed soul. What have you got there. Such pretty seashells."

"How many of them do you want?"

"Heavenly angels. Well. To tell the truth, one would be enough. These scoundrels only ask for a few rupees. But you'd accommodate me by leaving a few more if you don't mind. You see," he held up the bottle of brandy, "it costs an infernal fortune to get this stuff flown in on that bandit of an airline, and I think they drink half of it on the way. And I have other expenses."

I didn't inquire what these were. The upshot was that I left him a handful of the things, since he was such a helpful and cheerful fellow. It would also lighten my load; I could see that there wasn't going to be any Bahram to carry my suitcase from now on.

The sun went down abruptly behind the mountain to the west, and the air turned a piercing and silvery gray. Gresseth-Jones walked down to the warehouse with me. I carried the suitcase of course. Waiting in front of the door of the building was a battered Land Rover which had evidently once been a military vehicle; at least there were traces of khaki paint on it here and there, and a white blotch which, tracing out with my pencil several days later, I restored as a painted white star. Standing by it were my fellow passengers, a quartet of leather-colored fellows who wore white rags wrapped around their heads and dirty white garments which trailed to the ground. They all appeared to be carrying knives or other sharp weapons hidden in these garments, although I never actually caught sight of such. When one of them muttered something to his companion I recognized the voice.

"These are the fellows from the calaboose."

"You see, old man, these are chaps that have run amok one time too many. So we're transporting them, you see. Off the scene. We do that occasionally."

"Are you sure they won't be dangerous?"

"Oh no. They're harmless enough fellows. Just don't give them anything to drink, and don't talk to them about politics."

I had no idea what politics would be in Tuk or Kut. Perhaps it consisted of saying derogatory things about Gresseth-Jones. We all climbed in. The others paid no attention to me; no doubt they took me for another habitual criminal like themselves. Gresseth-Jones passed in my suitcase.

The engine started up and made quite a racket. The muffler system was defective. Gresseth-Jones had to raise his voice to be heard above it. "When you get there," he yelled, "I recommend calm, and lots of it. Don't lose your head. If you can keep your head when all about you are losing theirs . . . "

"Kipling," I shouted back.

The Land Rover went off with a jerk. After each time it stopped, the driver had to accelerate violently in order to break the tires loose from the sand. Gresseth-Jones raised his hand in a distant and indifferent way, and then turned and went back toward the bungalow, moving slowly and tilting a little to one side. He disappeared into the bungalow where the brandy was.

In this vehicle I traveled eastward over the mountains and desert for what seemed an endless time, although it was probably only a few days. Meals and sleep were irregular, and I had no way of keeping track of the days anyhow. My Seiko was not a calendar watch. With the canvas screens fixed into place it was semi-dark in the back of the Land Rover and I slept a good deal of the time. There was not much else to do. As for meals, these took place at totally random intervals. My fellow passengers had a store of pocket-bread into which they put millet sprouts, olives, and curds bought from the locals, who must have herded some sort of animals off behind the hills, although they kept them well out of sight. To drink, there was whey left over from making the curds. All this they freely shared with me, although it was still not clear whether they thought I was one of themselves or somebody else. I thought it best not to open my suitcase and reveal its contents, so I had nothing to offer except a half pack of Italian cigarettes, which were soon used up. I never exchanged more than two words with them. I never found out whether what they were speaking among themselves was Arabic or something else, perhaps Pushtu. Whenever I said "Salaam" to them they replied with something like "Djinni," which may have meant that I was a Devil, or merely "The Devil with it."

The driver of the Land Rover was a Turk named Fawvi who wore overalls and a dirty tarboosh. He smelled abominably, and perhaps in order not to smell himself, he incessantly smoked black Egyptian cigars. The odor of these wafted back into the rear of the Land Rover, where it mingled with the smell of Fawvi himself and with the less pungent but still peculiar odors of my fellow passengers.

Fawvi didn't seem to be armed, although he had a kind of scimitar which he kept propped up against the windshield, and used now and then to hack away at the thorny-brush when it impeded the progress of the Land Rover. Perhaps he could have chased off bandits with it too; he looked ferocious enough. He never spoke a word to me during our entire journey, although I had hoped to try out my Turkish with him. So far this trip was not proving to be very educational in the matter of languages. I had acquired a little Uqbari out of Captain Saǐd's dictionary, but I had learned only one word of the language spoken around Kut or Tuk, and that was Ga. The natives always insisted on speaking their version of English, if they knew a little. It was the curse of the serious-minded traveler.

One thing was certain, and that was that my fellow passengers did not speak the tongue of the land we were passing through. When they bought provisions from the natives, they communicated mainly by gesticulations, thumps on the chest, and fingers held up for calculations. After a day or two, I got out and engaged one of the locals in conversation, while my companions were occupied with this dumb-show.

"Where does the milk come from?"

He only grinned back at me.

I pointed to the curds and whey. "What kind of animal?" I made noises like a cow, a sheep, a goat.

"Iko."

He whinnied.

"Ah, horse." Since I had made a study of philology, I understood perfectly the development of the word from its Sanscrit origins through *hippos* to *equus*. Evidently *iko* had spun off somewhere in the middle of this process, and in some way the word had lodged up here in this remote corner of the world. Following this look-say technique, in only a few days I learned enough of this language to be able to prattle quite a bit of it to the people along the way who sold us things to eat. I never did learn what it was called, and in my own mind I thought of it by a word I had made up myself, Hippolytic. Its grammar was rudimentary, its vocabulary basically primitive Aryan or Urgermanisch. The words for mother, water, earth, sun, were only variations of those in Sanscrit. My fellow passengers didn't seem impressed by this linguistic achievement of mine. They conferred among themselves, glowered, pointed to the natives outside the Land Rover, and muttered "djinn." Evidently everyone was devils except themselves. I reflected, however, that *djinni* (plural *djinn*) was a cognate of Italian *genio*, French *génie*, so perhaps they were merely saying that I was a genius for picking up languages so quickly. I made no attempt to teach them Hippolytic. They were doing fine with their thumping and holding up fingers.

After several days of this we came to Asham, which was as far as the Land Rover could go. It was a good-sized town and I hoped to be able to find some other means of transportation there. It was the end of the journey for my four traveling companions. They seemed to be more or less at ease in the place and knew what to do with themselves, even though it wasn't their country. With knowing looks at each other, they disappeared into the bazaar, following along after a veiled lady who was carrying a purse over her hip. That was the last I saw of them.

Making inquiries, I was directed to a camel-drover and dealer who had set up shop in the courtyard of an inn. He saw immediately that I was a hopeless novice and sold me the worst camel in the place. I realized this only later; at the time I couldn't have told one of the mangy beasts from the other. I think I was influenced by the fact that my camel's name was Sylvia. At least the drover said that was her name, although it was not clear why she should have such a name; perhaps because she was a creature of the wilds. Female camels, I later learned, have far worse dispositions than the males, and the males are bad enough. Since he had no change for my Krugerrand, the drover threw in a cooking-pot, a bag or two of provisions, a bundle of firewood, and a stool made of three clubs and a triangle of leather that fastened to the top of them. I was rather pleased with this last item. It folded up to be loaded on Sylvia, and it rendered a kind of dignity to each of my campgrounds. When you have something to sit on, a piece of furniture, you are no longer a mere waif and wanderer on the face of the earth, you have established a place of residence, a little enclave of civilization to fend off the wilderness, if only temporarily. Finally the drover, in a burst of generosity, gave me a map, which he said had been tried and proven many times; it certainly looked as though it was several hundred years old.

It goes without saying that when all these things were loaded onto Sylvia—the suitcase on one side and the cooking-pot, the provisions, the firewood, and the camp-stool on the other to balance it—there was no room for me to ride. In any case, I doubted that I had the necessary skill, or that Sylvia was capable of supporting the extra weight. Along with Sylvia went a length of rope, ending in a ring that fastened in her nose. Perhaps it was this that made her so cross. And so we set out: I in the lead, then the length of rope, and Sylvia coming reluctantly on afterward.

The landscape ahead of me was formidable. After a half-day more of the usual desert I came up onto a dry and windy upland. Ahead of me I could see a range of snowclad peaks which I had to cross, through the Koni Pass, a notorious obstacle (it was called the Col Ducon in French) which I had heard rumors about in Asham and elsewhere. It took me several days to work my way up to the Koni, mainly because Sylvia was so uncooperative. Not only was she ugly, she was stubborn and vindictive. She was clever at divining what I wanted to do and then exerting every effort to prevent me from doing it. At times phlegmatic, at other times she was capable of the most unexpected and unpredictable acts of viciousness. She kicked, she bit, she sat down on me when I was trying to unload her, and should I turn my back on her for a minute she would lie down on her side so that her load slipped off. In the evening, after I had camped, she dexterously defecated in my cooking-pot while it was still over the fire.

"You ungrateful bitch," I told her, "if it were not for me, you would still be in Asham being beaten by the drover, instead of enjoying this delightful outing in the open."

Perhaps in response to this, she waited until the next time my back was turned and ate my map. I never beat her; I didn't believe in corporal punishment and anyhow I didn't think it would have any effect on her. Besides I didn't have anything to hit her with; I would have had to take apart my camp-stool and use one of its legs, and this was too much trouble. "You're lucky I don't have a goad," I told her. "The drover had a nice one, with a long rusty tip. I'm sorry now I didn't ask him for it." The fact that I was able to talk to Sylvia along the way, however, did relieve my solitude a little.

So we crossed the Koni—it was bitter kkkkold up there, and a boreal blast bored through the icy orifice of the col—and wound down, both of us slipping and tripping on the pebbles, onto the lunar and improbable terra incognita of the Bogi Plateau. This consisted for the most part of a desiccated alkali plain, white on the surface and intersected with black polygons where the dried mud showed through the cracks—it looked like the tessellated skin of a giraffe. Some salty grass, chartreuse-colored and tasting of licorice if you tried to chew it (we both did), sprang somehow from the lacerations of this lackluster landscape. At least it was level. The main problem was finding water. I grew quite skilled at this after a day or two. The thing was to look for vultures, and if you followed the vultures you came after a while to the corpses of foxes, jackals, hares, and other small fauna who had tried to drink the arsenical effluent of some puke-colored spring or other, and a little farther on you came to the spring itself. Of course we had to be careful not to drink too much of it ourselves, but we were smarter than the foxes; we only dampened our palates enough to soften the parched swelling of our tongues. Sylvia took a whole mouthful of it once, and I was about to tell her not to when she expertly squirted a thin but powerful stream of it at me, most of it hitting me in the eye. "Sylvia," I only told her mildly, "you have rotten table manners." I could appreciate her resentment; after all I was the one who was in charge of this expedition and who had brought both of us to this poisonous part of the world.

After perhaps another seven days or so (I had still lost count, or rather I had never regained it) we saw behind us unmistakable signs that we were not the only travelers on the plain. A cloud of white alkali-dust, trailing into the air like a feather, was following along steadily behind us, gaining a little hour by hour.

There was no chance that it was some troupe of wild beasts; its course and speed were too methodical. I stopped Sylvia, took down the suitcase, and removed a single Krugerrand. Then I looked around for some place to hide it, either on me or somewhere on Sylvia. I considered briefly anal insertion upon my own person, but changed my mind on reflecting that this was the most traditional of hiding places for small valuable objects and the first place anyone would look. There were no pockets in the burnoose, and the golden gleam of the coin would be instantly visible anywhere in my other possessions. In the end I decided to put it into Sylvia's vagina. I didn't think anyone was likely to disturb it there, even another camel, considering Sylvia's advanced age and her general bad temper. What she thought of this procedure I don't know. She did kick me while I was carrying out the insertion, but she did this anyhow whenever I came close to her.

When the dust-cloud finally closed in, toward nightfall, it transformed itself into a troupe of nomads, mounted on Asian ponies, with slant eyes and short strong legs. (If that sentence is a little ambiguous, Mr. Consul General, it is because I am tired and the light is bad in this place; I meant in fact to indicate that both the riders and their mounts had these features). There were a dozen or so of them and they were driving a dozen herd-horses along with them, as a kind of trotting dairy and butcher shop.

They rode along parallel to me for a while, and then the one in the lead called out "Hello there."

I smiled in a friendly way.

"Headed along toward Tush, are you?"

By this time my Hippolytic was fairly fluent. "Yes, I'm headed along this way, but I'm not sure where I'm going, because my camel ate my map."

"That's a shame about the map. Well, you're headed along toward Tush all right. It's a fairly decent sort of place. What do you intend to do when you get there?"

"Continue on toward the Mysterious Orient."

"A romantic sort of fellow, eh?"

We went on in this way, exchanging harmless badinage for a few days. They were a merry bunch. Apparently they had nothing better to do than trail along with me, singing folk songs and telling riddles among themselves and engaging in occasional conversation with me. After a while I got to know a good deal about their habits and way of life. They lived by drinking mares' milk and eating horsemeat steaks which they cooked by putting them under their saddles and galloping around on them all day. As far as I could tell, the horses ate the yellowish licorice-grass and extracted enough nourishment from it to grow quite fat and muscular. At night, when we camped, they shared their equine victuals with me, and it was a change from the boiled millet I had been living on now for a week. They took quite an interest in my suitcase, especially when they noticed that I took it off of Sylvia and used it as a pillow when I slept at night. Finally they began asking me all sorts of questions.

"What's in the suitcase?" inquired one, just to get the game started.

Another: "Perhaps you have a little girl-friend in there that you could take out and introduce to us."

A third: "No, it's probably full of oranges and sweet pears from the Vale of Sharon. Let's have some. We're all a bit thirsty."

The joker of the bunch, who was always telling improbable tales of one kind or another, had a theory that it contained the ashes of his grandmother. "She died three months ago, and at the village they told me that someone came and took away her ashes in a brown suitcase just like that." He grinned, pleased with himself at the preposterousness of this story.

"How can you have villages if you are nomads?"

"Well, we keep our grandmothers in villages."

"Maybe it's full of gold pieces," suggested one of his

companions, with heavy innuendo and exchanging glances with the others.

They discussed this among themselves. "How could it be full of gold pieces?"

"It's heavy as hell. I saw him tottering when he tried to lift it off of that sick old camel."

"It's a machine gun," I told them. "I may shoot you all."

"What's a machine gun?"

"A machine gun is a gun that's a machine. It just goes on shooting. You don't have to reload it."

They all looked at each other and then at me.

"What's a gun?"

"Never mind."

I went on trudging along, turning to give a tug to Sylvia, who thought she saw a tuft of grass under her legs.

"We'd better look into the suitcase anyhow," the leader decided, "just to be sure it isn't gold pieces."

"Where would a fellow like him get a lot of gold pieces?"

"Maybe he's Ali Baba."

"But there aren't forty of you," I pointed out.

"No, but we're pretty strong, and we've got these bubbahs," they said, pointing to the short sharp dirks which they used to cut steaks off their horses and for other domestic tasks.

"You're right," I told them, "I am Ali Baba, and my suitcase is full of gold pieces, and my friend the invisible sorcerer Al-Iqwar is lurking just behind my shoulder, waiting to change you all into wild asses."

"Gobo," they said—pointing to the grinning joker—"is an ass already. It wouldn't be much of a trick with him."

"Well, he'll change you all into wild asses. So I suggest we stop talking about what's in my suitcase, and go on in our friendly way like this for another mile or two, after which we can part, and you go your separate ways and I'll go mine."

"That's a good idea," they said, "but we think we'll take the suitcase anyhow."

"Don't forget Al-Iqwar."

"Well, supposing he does change us into wild asses. We can offer him half the gold pieces to change us back into nomads again."

"Isn't that a folklore motif?"

"You could look it up in Stith Thompson," they said. "Anyhow, we'll try it and see if Al-Iqwar has heard of the story."

"Where would I be all of this time?"

"Full of bubbah holes."

"Well, then maybe you'd better take the suitcase, if that would satisfy you," I conceded.

"We don't say it would satisfy us, but we'll take it."

They really were pleasant fellows. When they left they made me a present of two horsemeat steaks, still slightly warm. Then, with a chorus of merry farewells and hoots to encourage their horses, they wheeled around and turned back to the west, following their own clearly visible tracks in the alkali that stretched off to the horizon. As soon as you stepped in this whitish stuff the mud under the surface came through and you left a black mark in it. That was no doubt how they had tracked me so effortlessly. Why they accompanied me for three days and then turned back in the same way they had come I don't know. Maybe they had gone back to the grandmother-village to see if anybody else had died. I continued on my way, after stopping to rearrange the remainder of my possessions—the cooking-pot, the provisions, the firewood, and the stool—so that they balanced on Sylvia's back.

It was only a day or so after this that I came to Tush, a good-sized collection of mud huts and the last town before the border. I took a room for myself at the inn, and Sylvia was put up in the stable, which was called a *kvransrai* in Hippolytic. It was with a little thrill of recognition that, after a moment, I identified this as the word *caravansary*. I really *was* having an adventure, I told myself, in spite of all my hardships. In fact I had almost forgotten them now that I was put up comfortably at the inn.

At the police station in Tush, a larger mud hut distinguished from the others only because it had a flag in front of it on a pole, I attempted to report the theft of my Krugerrands to the police commissioner. But he was more interested in pursuing the possibility that I was a criminal myself, probably because I was easier to catch than the nomads, since I was seated cross-legged on a rug directly in front of him. (I had left behind the part of the world where chairs were customary, and I wasn't allowed to bring my stool into the police station.) The commissioner was barefoot, clad in a kind of dhoti and intricately wrapped turban, both immaculately white. About halfway down his nose he wore a pair of old-fashioned steel spectacles which had somehow found their way to this part of the world from the distant west. No squatting on the floor for him; he was supported in a kind of sitting-hammock slung from the ceiling, in which he swung slowly and thoughtfully back and forth like some sort of judiciary Foucault pendulum.

"You say they took a lot of gold coins. Where did you get these gold coins?"

"I traded them out of a merchant named H. Karagian."

"Traded them, eh? What did you give him for them?"

"I could make you an inventory if you like. A pair of tennis shorts, some underwear, some German condoms, and a lot of travelers checks."

"What would be the exact value of the merchandise you traded him including the travelers checks?"

"Oh, about equal to the gold coins, I would say. I think I got a little the better of the deal."

"You sound like a rather dubious character to me. I don't really understand your story at all. It sounds to me like something you just made up here on the spur of the moment."

"Why then would I come to you complaining that I've been robbed?"

"I don't know, I'm trying to figure that out, too. You've got some sort of dubious scheme going on here, that's clear, and I mean to get to the bottom of it."

In short, I had a hell of a time getting away unscathed from this police commissioner, and I wonder if you, Distinguished Signor Consul, might take some measures to see if something can't be done about such effrontery to honest Venetian subjects in a country which is a neighbor, and a small and defenseless one, of the largest and most powerful Empire in the world. At least, a tactful word through diplomatic channels, hinting at the disparity in military power between the two nations, might be enough to cause the removal from office of this particular individual, who let me go only after suggesting, unsuccessfully, that I might make him a present of my Seiko wristwatch in order to stimulate him into a search for the criminals. I was left with the impression—one that I have had, to tell the truth, in other parts of the world as well—that the police arm of the government in Tush was chiefly a system of tax collection for the benefit of the police.

I spent the night at the inn, in a reasonable degree of comfort. The next morning I extracted the gold coin from Sylvia's vagina and gave it to the innkeeper in return for my night's lodging and two meals, receiving in change a large pile of paper money called piasters, which were the most filthy currency I had ever seen in my life. The bills were the size of theater tickets and printed on something resembling toilet paper. On each bill was stamped with a crude rubber stamp, "Not valid in time of war." Since I had heard loud screams and the gallop of hooves during the night, I assumed that there was always more or less a war going on in these parts. I kept the piasters anyhow, even though I suspected they were worthless. On the whole I had a pleasant time in Tush and left refreshed, in spite of my encounter with the police commissioner. It occurred to me several days later that perhaps the nomads were in the pay of Gresseth-Jones. If so I really didn't begrudge him the Krugerrands; he probably had more need of them than I did.

Sylvia too seemed in good spirits; she only bit me once while I was loading her and her stomach was fat from the licorice-straw they had fed her in the kvransrai. We set off in our customary manner, soon leaving the collection of mud huts behind in the thin sunshine. The terrain now changed again. There was more rising country, and we had to cross over a kind of escarpment tilted to the west, like a careened caravel, that was the natural boundary separating the Bogi Plateau from the Empire. We were still a long way from the border, however. The trail went on through brown hills and ravines, which were dry at this time of the year—a shame, not only because we were both thirsty, but because I had looked forward with excitement to the moment when I would see water running to the east rather than to the west. Water, however, was easier to find here among the hills than it was on the Bogi, and it was of somewhat better quality. Every half day's march or so there was a spring; we formed the habit of pausing at one to rest in the heat of the day, and then camping at the next spring for the night. The campgrounds I remembered by the names I gave to the springs, descriptive of the waters they contained: Quinine Tonic, Venetian Canal,

Baden Baden, Cat Piss, and so on. Sylvia didn't seem to notice the difference among them, although I would have expected a camel to be a connoisseur in matters of waters. At least she didn't spit out any of them at me as she had the alkali water on the plateau. I was growing rather fond of Sylvia. Her independence of spirit had a certain dignity to it. She disdained the food that I found for her now, and instead ate snakes, which she found for herself. Once she was bitten by a viper on the knee and limped for four days, but she stopped whenever she saw that I was watching; she was too proud.

Then one night we camped in a grassy dell with the hills all around, and a bountiful supply of rotten tree-limbs for firewood. I was pleased at having found a particularly nice spring, the best one, in fact, since we had left Tush. The water was delicious, as clear as the finest Baccarat and slightly pétillant. I was a little puzzled by the fact that no one else seemed to have camped there; there were no signs of previous fires, and in fact no evidence that animals had come to the place to drink. In the arid regions of the world, when a fox or a ferret finds a good spring after several days of searching, he usually leaves a souvenir to show how pleased he was with the place. Meditating over this ecological riddle, I lay down and went to sleep. I was very tired.

I soon found out the curse that lay over the campground. A little short of midnight I awakened to find myself covered with hordes of giant beetles as large as toads. In a manner of seconds they had cut every bit of my burnoose into pieces the size of postage stamps, as skillfully as seamstresses with their scissors. One of them even severed the strap of my Seiko wristwatch, and in the flickering embers of the campfire I caught a glimpse of him waddling away, dragging it after him into the darkness. Meanwhile his companions, having disposed of the burnoose, set about attacking the flesh underneath. There was a sensation as though I were being given a hundred and ten tetanus injections all at once. I leaped up in agony and flung myself into the spring. But the creatures still clung to me with their razor-sharp pincers, and I had to get out of the water and pluck them off one by one as best I could, in the dim glow of the embers from my cook-fire. The last one had its strong mandible fixed into the very end of my reproductive apparatus. With a grimace of pain I removed him and flung him into the night.

When I had them all off, I made a torch by lighting a tree-branch in the embers and started surveying the damage to myself and my expedition. The remaining beetles I was able to chase away easily enough by flourishing the torch at them. There was no sign of the precisely particulated burnoose, however; they evidently carried off the fragments for some purpose of their own. On the other side of the fire I saw Sylvia doing a kind of four-legged tap-dance, effectively dislodging the beetles from her legs and trampling them under her large horny hooves. My provisions I had hung from a tree-branch; they were intact. The main damage from the attack, apart from the pain, was that I was now stark naked. Luckily, before I lay down I had taken off the red-and-white checked scarf and dropped it onto the camp-stool. The beetles had evidently been unable to climb up its slick clubs. I wound the scarf around my loins and between my legs and tucked it in. It would do for the purposes of modesty, although it didn't do much to keep me warm. Sylvia and I thought it best to leave this doomed place immediately and set out along the trail in the pitch blackness. We stumbled now and then, and once we both fell down and landed in a heap with Sylvia on top. But after only four hours or so there was a little light in the east. The experience with the beetles was a painful one, but I thought I learned a lesson. I told myself: this campground has been there for five thousand years, during which a thin but constant stream of travelers has passed this way. If there is still firewood lying on the ground, there is some reason for it.

In this way, after a few more days, I arrived at the border of Cathay, dusty, hot, thirsty, half-starved with only a handful of millet left in my provision-bag, naked, sunburned, covered with beetle-bites, my sandals in shreds, and my skin abraded from the sharp sand that had found its way into every crevice of my body. The border itself was not very grandiose. I don't know what I had expected. There was a gate made of two tree-trunks with a curved lintel over them high in the air, and on either side of this a line was scratched into the dirt for a few yards until it disappeared into the stony earth. The place was a military outpost more than a town. The improvements consisted of a barracks, a stone house with a stone chimney, fairly comfortable, for the officer in charge, and a stockade full of sheep for victuals. Finally, another small and inconspicuous building that I was to be introduced to shortly. At the gate a bored soldier was standing with his legs crossed, leaning against one of the posts. He immediately put me under arrest.

The officer in charge of the place (his name, as I later found out, and as I have already reported to you, Most Exalted Signor Consul, was and still is Lieutenant Mu) was of several minds what to do with me. Entrance into the Empire by any foreigner was strictly forbidden, and even to be caught roaming the border regions was prima facie evidence of spying. Moreover, once you entered the Empire there were even stricter laws against leaving, and I had entered the Empire when I was dragged through the gate by the soldier. The possibilities including executing me summarily, sending me back where I had come from, and as a compromise holding me in custody while he wrote off for instructions to the capital of Xanadu, which had to be done on a special form involving fourteen copies of rice-paper. This last procedure, if I understood the language right—I was still a little slow on the calendar terms—would require a wait of eight months or so, or perhaps it was only eight weeks.

Lieutenant Mu was a reasonable fellow of a philosophical turn of mind. He appeared, to judge from his demeanor, which was noble and weary, to be a person of good family and education who had, perhaps, been exiled to this post from the capital for some unspeakable misdemeanor. He interviewed me in the central room of his house, wearing a yellow silk skirt, a tunic fastened with a dozen tiny buttons, and a pillbox hat with a single tassel on it to indicate his rank of lieutenant.

He called for a cup of tea, and offered me one as well. We sat cross-legged on the floor at opposite ends of the room. His questions were the regulation ones, but the manner of his putting them was bored and perfunctory.

"What are you doing roaming around on the border anyhow? You're up to no good, that's one thing certain."

"I wasn't roaming around on the border. I came straight to this place and I want to continue on to the capital. Let me put a question to you. What are you fellows up to anyhow in Cathay that you're so anxious for foreigners not to see it?"

"I'm the one that puts the questions. What financial means or other valuables do you possess?"

"You can ask your soldiers. They've already pawed me over and taken away everything I owned. A red-and-white checked shawl, a camel, and a handful of millet."

I should have explained that by this time the shawl had

been confiscated and I was provided with a kind of loose baggy poncho consisting of a six-foot circle of oilcloth with a hole in it, the traditional jail garb in Cathay, as I later found out.

"You forgot the stool. A mendacious statement under oath." He made a note. "You came all the way with no further resources?"

"All what way?"

"Are you affiliated with the political or military service of any foreign power?"

"If I were, what could I do? Hit you in the chops with my bare fist?"

"What are your reasons for wishing to enter the Empire?"

"Touristical."

"Tourism is not allowed in the Empire. Anyhow tourists have financial means."

"So did I, before I was robbed by friendly nomads."

"Look here, whoever you are—I can't really believe your name is Polo—I'll be frank with you. I don't know what in the hell to do with you. The trouble is that there's no precedent because this sort of thing happens so infrequently. The last time somebody tried to cross this border illegally was in 1360. That was twenty years ago, for God's sake, when I was still a boy in school. The border code has been changed three times since then. The best thing is to write to the capital for instructions. In the meanwhile I'm going to put you into the kar-shel. You can't get into very much trouble there."

The kar-shel is the small inconspicuous building I have previously mentioned, which I noticed on my arrival in the place. It is a rounded and oblong structure something like a Dutch oven, made of native stone with lots of cement. The only opening is a door at the bottom two feet or so high and twice as wide. I had to crawl on my hands and knees to get into the place whereupon the soldiers clanked shut the grill of iron bars. And there I was and still am. The ceiling was too low for me to stand up; if I sat up I couldn't see out; and to see out I had to lie down with my head propped on my elbow and look out through the iron bars. I remember reading once that an ape in a zoo was taught to draw, and drew a picture of the bars of his cage. I wasn't however, provided with any drawing materials. At night the cold wind from the mountains blew into the place, and in the middle of the day, with the sun beating down on it, it was as hot as Hades. I remembered those wretches in the calaboose in Tuk or Kut that I had felt so superior to. Where were they now? Probably reveling in the fleshpots of Asham.

I found a sharp little rock and made a mark on the inside of my domicile. In this way I would keep track of the days. Next I cast about for some means of amusing myself. Directly opposite the low hole in the Dutch oven, I found, was the sheep-stockade, and there was always something going on there. Either the sheep were courting each other, or they were engaged in territorial disputes and butting-skirmishes, or a soldier would come to slaughter one. For this last purpose a scaffold of timbers the height of a man had been erected near the gate of the stockade. A soldier came along armed with a knife and selected an old ram from the dozen or so sheep who were quarreling in the stockade. With the help of a boy, he tied the ram up on the scaffold by his hind legs. Then he got out his knife and cut the throat with a patient sawing motion, since the knife was not very sharp. After the blood stopped spurting out, the soldier cut a small incision in the ram's ankle and began to blow vigorously, as though he were inflating a balloon. In a half an hour, red and puffing, he had inflated the sheepskin free of the carcass. He then removed the skin by sawing along the insides of the limbs and belly. In the end, the pelt came off as easily as though he were removing an overcoat from the animal. The boy gravely noted all these steps so that some day he could do it himself.

The soldier poured a bucket of water over the carcass and cut it into pieces. Finally he wrapped everything up in the sheepskin, and he and the boy went off with it toward the barracks. Perhaps the ram was for Lieutenant Mu's dinner. It would be a little tough, but probably they had recipes. As for the pelt, it was no doubt used to make one of the sheepskin jackets the soldiers wore over their silk uniforms to protect them from the mountain blasts.

All this was very entertaining. It occurred to me that this might also be the local means of executing suspected spies, since there didn't seem to be any other apparatus for capital punishment in sight. In this way the tomorrows crept in their petty pace from day to day, and I managed to avoid insanity and was even "not unhappy" as I put it to myself. I practiced my Cathayan with the occasional soldiers who hunkered down before the kar-shel to peer at the curiosity inside, I scratched theorems from quantum physics on the wall with the sharp rock, and I composed a rondel in Venetian at the expense of Lieutenant Mu, ending:

> Remembering Zanadu, the sound of flutes,
> And love by plashing fountains,
> He drinks his tea and gazes at the mountains.

I had no idea whether there were either flutes or plashing fountains in Zanadu, but the rhyme worked out nicely. It was not so jingly in the original.

I soon worked out an economy with my jailers. Every day they gave me a plate of food, and every day I gave them a pail of excrement in return. They were decent enough fellows and only doing their job. They hadn't asked to be sent to this God-forsaken place, although most of them had been guilty only of small misdemeanors, such as speaking disrespectfully to their grandfathers, or killing the sacred Shan-Tu roaches that sometimes took up residence in private kitchens. If it was true that they showed very little concern for my dignity and comfort, not to mention my civil rights, this was because most of them were a long way from home and had had few advantages in life. They ate my camel without even asking me. Poor Sylvia! It had been a rotten life for her, on the whole. No one had ever truly cared for her, and instead of love, like so many females she had received only coin. As for my piasters, the soldiers used them for toilet paper, one piece at a time. These lasted for quite a while, and when they were gone they went back to their former practices.

A hundred and eleven days passed in this way (I was still making scratches on the wall) before word came on my case from the capital. Lieutenant Mu called me in for another interview, and waited patiently while I, with great savor, drank the cup of tea he offered me. Then, without losing his aplomb, he threw a small folded wad of rice-paper across the room at me.

"What do you make of this?"

I unfolded the paper. There was no address and no signature. It was true that the paper bore the Imperial watermark, but it could have been written by any lackey or bureaucrat in the capital. On it, in the ceremonial old-fashioned T'ang Dynasty script, I read: "Signor Polo, the subject of your communication of the 15th Persimmon, has not yet arrived in Xanadu to present his credentials, and therefore no action can be taken on your request."

"It says," I told him, "that I haven't got there yet."

"Polo, I'm at my wit's end. What am I going to do with you? If I leave you in that kar-shel any longer you're going to die of inanition, and then I'll be accused of mistreatment of prisoners."

I respectfully suggested to him that these were his problems and not mine; I certainly hadn't initiated them and I would be more than happy to see them come to an end.

"Put it this way. What would you do if you were in my place? I mean, suppose that I, as a Cathayan, came to Venice and were arrested as a suspected spy. What would happen to me exactly?"

"In the first place, instead of being confined in a wretched bake-oven such as you have here, you would be provided with quarters in the Prigioni, a magnificent gothic building constructed by Antonio Da Ponte, who also designed the Rialto Bridge, and connected to the Ducal Palace by another well-known architectural attraction, the— "

"I know, the Bridge of Sighs."

I looked around to see if there were some *National Geographics* in the crude stone house, but there was nothing except a few books of poems and the ledger in which Mu kept track of the soldiers' pay, sheep-slaughterings, and the arrests of suspected spies.

"It's quite nice in the Prisons," I went on. "You can have your meals brought in if you can afford to pay for them." I hoped this might be a hint for him to improve the cuisine a little in my own bake-oven.

"Yes, but how would my case be settled?"

"Oh, it wouldn't be settled. You'd be taken back and forth to the Ducal Palace now and then, via the Bridge of Sighs, to be interviewed by the Inquisitors. This is called Putting the Question and they have special devices. Everything you say is written down in a large book they have, and then they take you back to your cell."

"And after that?"

"I don't know. I suppose you could complain to your consul."

"Well, why don't you complain to *your* consul?"

"I might, if I had any writing materials. If I scratched it on the walls of the kar-shel with my sharp rock, you'd have to send the kar-shel to Xanadu and then you wouldn't have any place to keep me in."

"You mean there are no writing materials in there?"

"There's nothing."

"Nothing?" He seemed incredulous.

"Well, there's a pail." It occurred to me that he had never inspected the kar-shel very carefully himself. He had just told the soldiers to put people in it, without going along with them to see what this amounted to.

"Well, take this pen. It's my own and the only one I've got. Heaven help you if you lose it or break the nib."

He handed me the vulture plume aforementioned in this communication, along with some rice-paper and a leather pouch of sticky ink. And so here I am, Illustrious Signor Consul, back in the kar-shel which I have inhabited so long now that it seems almost a home to me, hunkered down with my rear in the air and inditing this petition with the pail turned upside down for a writing-desk—the slight odor emanating from these papers may serve to give you some concrete notion of my predicament. My posture, an inefficient one for serious literary composition, is dictated by the low ceiling of the kar-shel and by the necessity of getting close enough to the iron-barred door to throw a little light on what I am doing. I am sure all this is affecting my style, which is tending toward the pathetic and extravagant—the farthest thing possible from my own preferences and the inclinations of my temperament.

Worst of all, I am not sure I have the address right, or your own title, Magnificent Sir Consul General, as I have indicated in other places in this writing. How this message is to be carried to Xanadu I have no idea. Perhaps Lieutenant Mu will not send it to the capital at all, but only stick it into his ledger as evidence, should it be needed later, of the absolute insanity of his prisoner. For how can one hope to succeed in a petition when he does not know the name, the correct title, or the address of the person to whom he is writing, and cannot even be sure of his existence? Such metaphysical doubts, quite at odds with my normal rational personality, have begun to assail me lately. Perhaps I have imagined all this, I tell myself, or perhaps I am only a character in a work of fiction I am writing down on this rice-paper in order to while away the hours in this hopeless place. Or perhaps—and this notion now begins to float in my mind as though I were awakening from a dream, or falling into one—I myself am that Venetian emissary to the court of Xanadu to whom I am attempting to write.

LITTLE EDDY

It all began, no doubt, when my mother named me Edgar. Edward, Edmund, Edwin—these might serve as names for normal and happy human beings. But Edgar—no, something is wrong, there is a gritty growl toward the end, and even the first syllable is transformed by the g that follows into a kind of dull thump, as of something valuable falling to the floor and partially crushing itself. The name has no class. It is difficult to whisper in the transports of love. All of its diminutives are ludicrous. It encourages its owner to sign his middle name as well and thus go around with three names, a ridiculous affectation. It has too many consonants and an insufficient number of vowels. It is pronounced with the mouth entire open, leaving one vulnerable. It is impossible to incorporate into a poem and has no known rhymes. It is easily taught to talking birds, for the purpose of mocking its owner. In fact, some birds can say it without being taught at all, which gives you an idea of its elegance.

Believe it or not, I have never met another Edgar in all my born days. There is something fateful about this. Surely there must be a few other Edgars around. I would have been pleased enough, for example, to meet the creator of Tarzan, or that quaint and queer village poet who wrote the *Spoon River Anthology*. Was there ever a politician named Edgar—a chief of state—a director of companies? Does anyone know of an Edgar who was perhaps first to photograph the elusive quark, or who named a new flower? Even a Dwight or a Ronald could become President of the United States, even an Edsel could command an industrial empire. But Edgar? It is the name of a murderer, or a murderee. Never have I done either of these things; but the rest is bad enough. So much for prologue.

Now, for a while this is going to be a more or less conventional autobiography in the Dickensian manner, beginning "I was born" and going on to describe my early upbringing and so forth. I was born in 1943 in a small frame bungalow in South Pasadena, at 3010 Oxley Street, a rather shabby neighborhood. Nevertheless my family had a time-honored, although rather nebulous, tradition of distinction. My ancestry was Irish on my father's side, the usual "Irish, Scotch, and English" on my mother's side. The Sigourney family, according to legend, had once possessed a castle in County Cork, but had been forced to emigrate to America by the potato famine. I don't know why people who lived in a castle would need potatoes. At any rate this legend, like a dim archetypal memory, was passed along from generation to generation and served to sustain the family ego during its various adversities in the New World. As a child, in my private thoughts, I was able to generate an image of this heritage with an eidetic clarity. The castle stood on an imposing headland with the surf beating on the rocks below. Through the mists a maiden appeared on the battlements, clad in white, her long hair flowing in the wind, seeming to gaze into the distance for something. A solitary rider in black wound his way over the greenish-black meadow under the lowering clouds. Then he disappeared into the dark portal under the battlements, and his place in the movie-screen of my imagination was taken by a saddened Mother-Figure, also clad in white, whose face was indistinguishable in shadow but whose lineaments were marked by the unmistakable signs of grief. Wavering in slow motion, as ethereal and substanceless as a cloud, she floated along over the meadow after the rider until she too disappeared in the shadowy gulf of the portal. There were no other characters in my little drama; the cast confined to this triangle. The wind bent the grass and moaned over the convolutions of the old stones. What happened inside? This knowledge was forbidden me; in some way the x-ray of my imagination could not penetrate through the walls to the interior of that isolated and mossy old pile where, perhaps, some wandering minstrel had once sounded that same harp that rang in Tara's hall.

Perhaps if I had so vivid and so pictorial an imagination, with such a flair for the romanesque, it was because both my parents were actors. My father, Edmund Sigourney, even enjoyed a certain celebrity as a romantic lead before he took to drinking, about the time I was born, and found himself relegated to bit parts and dubbing voices in French films. He disappeared from sight before I was old enough to be aware of him. It was never made quite clear to me what happened to him; perhaps he entered a sanitarium to be treated for his addiction and died there, or perhaps he emerged after a time and spent the rest of his life alternating between alcoholism cures and the ignominious tasks that the film industry was willing to confer on such unreliable human derelicts. To my knowledge he never made any attempt to establish contact with my mother and me, but I don't think it would be fair to say he "deserted" his family. I imagine he simply took to the lifeboat, seeing that the ship was sinking. I was a frail and fretful child and my mother was a chronic invalid, suffering from weak lungs and a low resistance to infectious diseases. Of her I have a vivid but somewhat blurry memory, deriving for the most part, probably, from hearing other people talk about her, or from the glimpses I caught of her in later years in late-night films on TV. She played ingenue parts, even at thirty, and there was something ethereal and insubstantial about her, a ghost-like fragility, that suited her for roles in films with names like *The Haunted Manor* or *Bride of the Werewolf*. Yet some of my recollections of her are direct and even deeply sensuous. I *sense* rather than see her bending over my crib or my infantile bed; a voice as thin as a thread, with a pitiful catch in it, breaks out or sobs, "My Edgar!", and I am caught up in an enveloping warm embrace so fierce that I feel my tiny breath expelled from my body. There is an odor of talcum and lilac. I am pressed against her bosom, soft and bifurcated, and I am aware of every delicate bone in that part of her that encloses me. This embrace continues for a considerable time, perhaps a minute, during which I am unable to breathe. I feel at the same moment a deep sensual gratification and a terror: she wishes to take me with her! Of course at that age, a child in the cradle, I had no idea; and yet did I perhaps guess? Or is this only the cynical veil of interpretation that later wisdom casts over the infantile memory?

At any rate she went on her voyage without me, either finding that I was unwilling to accompany her or that she herself was too weak to bear me with her. I believe it was an attack of pneumonia, followed close on bronchitis, that carried her off; at least I remember a family friend, when I was a child, telling me "how your poor mother coughed." Winged seraphs bore her away, I guess, or else some underpaid employee of a funeral home, such as I myself later became. Her professional name was Mae Meadows. A lovely name, I think. It was she who had me christened Edgar Sigourney; a fateful decision, as it later developed, and one that no doubt had its own due part in my destiny.

And so I set out in life, an orphan at two—exactly like David Copperfield, except that I was even younger and somewhat less healthy. Luckily I had high-born relatives. A cousin of my mother, Javier Ramspeck, owned a department store in downtown Los Angeles and had a large and expensively furnished house in Hancock Park. He came from a wealthy branch of the family and had been a Rhodes Scholar, a member of the Board of Regents of the University of California, a director of the United Fund, and I don't know what else. His wife Frances, called Fanny by intimates, had taken a fancy to me even before my mother died. And indeed there was a good deal to take a fancy to, in spite of my sickliness and my pervading air of melancholy (we are talking about a child of two!), or perhaps because of these very qualities. As depicted in a photograph of the epoch, in ludicrous rompers which don't correspond to my personality at all, I am an emaciated little elf with two enormous eyes and a tiny mouth which I never opened at all. I seem wiser than my years, and no doubt I was. A wise child is one that knows his own father, and even in my playpen I knew that these surrogate progenitors were spurious. Let's go back to that photograph again. My attention had fallen solely on my own image, egotist that I am. But there they are; I am sitting on Fanny's lap; her hand, like a pale lotus, lies negligently between my thin outspread legs, and standing behind the sofa (preferring perhaps to put a piece of heavy furniture between himself and so trite a domestic scene), is her esteemed spouse, a beefy figure who looks strong enough to cow a whole building full of floorwalkers into selling people things they don't want. This bellicose stance was remarkable in one so thoroughly civilian. (It was wartime of course, but the department store magnate did not participate; he was 4-F, hopelessly incapacitated by wealth). Fanny is a dark-eyed woman in her thirties, prim, quick, and beautiful, giving a bird-like impression of intelligence. She is wearing a kind of loose peignoir, a silk affair printed with flowers that has slipped from one shoulder slightly to reveal the fine bonework of her upper body. She gazes straight into the camera, her chin lifted a little, confident, one feels, of her control over the affections and behavior, not only of the waif on her lap, but of the larger and more formidable male figure looming behind the sofa. Hello there, Mr. and Mrs. Ramspeck! I still have the photograph, in a velvet frame, in the drawer where I keep my underwear.

As soon as I could pronounce anything I was instructed to call my stepfather Javier and my stepmother Belle-Maman. She, Mrs. Ramspeck, Fanny, Belle-Maman, had a great affection for me, but she didn't fancy the role of motherhood and refused to have anything to do with such a vapid and primordial American vocable as Mom. She was a Bennington graduate, a servant of liberal causes, and later an active figure in Los Angeles society, such as it was. She treated me not as a child but as a tiny knowing man, one of the many people with whom she had close affections. She kissed me frequently and profusely and always patted me between the legs after she had checked to be sure my pants were buttoned. Perhaps she wished to see whether her caresses were having any effect. In any case she was disappointed, because such a phenomenon could hardly have occurred before I was twelve or so, and by that time I had graduated to pants with zippers and could check such things for myself.

But we have to jerk back and forth in time a little here, since that is the way the memory works. If we go into reverse, back to the point where I was three or so, we find that in those days Belle-Maman often lazed in her room in the morning after Javier had gone off to work, and would invite me in from my adjacent nursery to clamber around in her large satin bed. There she would lie, like Goya's Maya with one arm around the back of her head, watching me with grave amusement as I crawled about to explore, first, the expensive satin pillows and bedsheets of pastel pink, and then her own person, in a matching gown of pinkish lace pellucid enough to reveal darker patches and spots here and there through the flimsy stuff. Up and down her I would go, investigating interesting protuberances and sliding downhill again to thrust my little head into whatever recesses and concavities I happened to encounter on my way. "Can you give us a kiss?" I could; and then off to explore more Cyclop's Caves and rounded Mount Everests. Such adventures would end, usually, with my tiring of the game and crawling to rest in the crook of her shoulder, at just the right angle so that by bending a little she was able to kiss my small pale brow, and that I on the other hand could reach up to explore the delicacies of her aristocratic face with my fingers still so tiny that they could penetrate not only the corners of her mouth, but the chaste and pure pink orifice of her nostril, as perfect as the calyx of a flower.

In short we had a rich sentimental life in those idyllic and clandestine years, Belle-Maman and I, even though I was too immature to be capable of any gross mechanical fulfillment of these embraces we exchanged, and indeed had only the vaguest idea of what this would have entailed if I had been capable of it. And yet, even if I had possessed these larger weapons of love, it would have made little difference in our affections. I would have been like some general of the ancient world, a Hannibal or Caesar, provided with a modern cannon; I would have pursued the same tactics and enjoyed the same victories, and only the weaponry would have changed. In every way except this crassly physical sense we were lovers. We called each other by pet names and offered shy gifts to each other: I a daisy wrenched clumsily from the garden, bruised and half-wrecked but no less valuable in her eyes and mine; and she some sweetmeat which she would insert into my mouth with her own hand, allowing her fingers to linger for an instant while I cleansed them of their traces of sugar with a small but extraordinarily prehensile pink tongue. Her term of endearment for me, from the time when I was still too young to talk, was Popo. This was first intended to designate my behind, then, by the rule of synecdoche, was expanded to include my whole person and identity. Her customary greeting, when I was toddling around still scarcely able to babble, was "How's my little Popo?", accompanied by a light tap on my bottom. (She was interested in that part of me too). Her little Popo was just fine, and I reciprocated, when she lifted me to carry me blithely about the house on her hip, by palpating with my tiny fingers a bosom that corresponded almost exactly in its contours and its dimensions to that part of me that fascinated her so much, except that the twin protuberant convexities in her case were somewhat farther apart. To this she invariably responded with a sibylline smile and a faint flush of the cheeks.

Yet we all grow older, as is well known, and as we do so our erotic practices change and so does our sense of our own personal dignity and independence. When I was nine or so it began to occur to me that there was an element of the degrading, even of the ridiculous, in this pet name she applied so casually to me. The part of the body it referred to was a delicate one, and moreover it was the part that was affixed to the oval pink seat in Belle-Maman's bathroom—which I also shared; Javier had his own off the hall—for a daily procedure which was offensive to me in its very essence, and which also had its own whimsical name in our family vocabulary. I pondered (to tell the truth it was in there that I pondered, since it was there that the subject came to mind) and plotted a rebellion against this callous tyranny of love, this reducing of the whole to the part that I found so demeaning. And so, shortly after, there occurred the following little drama. I, proceeding into Belle-Maman's room still in my pajamas—which, as I remember, were yellow and printed all over with the effigy of a well-known movieland duck—was greeted with the usual "How's my little Popo?" and the accompanying caress. After the hand had patted me I shrank back, made a little moue of melancholy, and caused my lower lip to quiver slightly; I was already adept at such stageplay.

"Belle-Maman . . ."

"Yes, my sweet."

"I'd rather you didn't . . ."

"What, Popo dear?"

"Refer to my ass."

Her reaction, after a moment of thought, was a private and controlled little smile. Then she said, turning half away and allowing her glance to trail coyly over her shoulder, "But it's so delicious."

I couldn't find the words to tell her that it was not the caress I objected to, but the term applied to the part caressed. I began to fear that, in objecting to the nomenclature, I had deprived myself of the affection that accompanied it, and I cast about for some means of remedying the damage. With a true lover's instinct I abandoned words and sought to right matters with an embrace. But there was an awkwardness; since she had turned coquettishly away from me, when I wrapped my arms around her I found myself embracing exactly that part of her that I objected to when she referred to my own. She was more adept and practised; she was only playing with me. After leaving me in this awkward posture for a second or two, she twisted lightly in my arms so that her frontal aspect was presented to my gaze. Falling to my knees (I was a big boy now), I buried my face into the depression it found for itself somewhat below the waist of her loose and flowing silken wrapper. I felt a sense of warmth and forgiveness; she evidently felt something even more intense, since the tremor that passed through her frame and vibrated on for some time, like a signal from a distant earthquake, left her hot-faced and breathing heavily, although still smiling. She pulled me to one side and stroked my cheek lightly.

"Naughty Belle-Maman," she said after a moment.

I only continued to stare at her, uncomprehending.

"This will be our little secret, won't it?"

"Secret?"

"We wouldn't want to make Javier angry, would we?"

"We wouldn't?"

"No, we wouldn't, because then he might make us stop, and I wouldn't be able to kiss my little—I'm sorry." She could barely keep from laughing. "My little—Eddy anymore."

I didn't care much for this name either, but I kissed her when she bent down to my level. So our little quarrel ended, if that was what it had been.

I never again used such a vulgarity in her presence, and indeed all my life I have had a dislike for coarse language and coarse thoughts. This in part I can attribute to Belle-Maman and her superior culture, and in part to a natural refinement and delicacy of sentiment that, in any case, I would eventually have discovered in my own temperament. For her part, she quickly forgave me, and no doubt in her own mind she secretly accused her husband of having transmitted the offending term to me. And indeed it was a marvel where I acquired it, in so sheltered and decorous a household—but in reality it was Mr. Grimespan, the handyman who was called in to fix things like broken windows and leaky water-taps, and who informed me, among other things, that my esteemed stepfather the captain of commerce "didn't know his ass from a hole in the ground" (or, variorum, "from the Grand Canyon"), and that Belle-Maman was "going around with her ass in a sling" because her husband wouldn't give her a thousand dollars for a silver sable stole. He also referred to my surrogate parents as "your Ant-Fanny" (producing this distorting by a subtle shift of emphasis to the first syllable) and "old Ramspecker." The first of these sobriquets I resented hotly, although silently. The second I quickly made my own and cherished in my private thoughts as a recompense against the many indignities I endured from the gross and vital tyrant.

The house in Hancock Park was in Florentine villa style, two stories high with a tile roof and overhanging eaves, and cypresses in the garden around a pool where two lazy carp alternatively snapped at each other and swam indolently around through the lily-pads. Inside, the floors were all marble or terrazzo, and devoid of carpets which Belle-Maman contended were middle-class. The floors were cold to small feet, which was one reason—a minor one—why I was so willing to climb onto her bed in the morning. My stepparents entertained a great deal, and such occasions I was banished to the nursery—later converted to "Eddy's room" by removing the crib and the authentic Peter Rabbit lithographs and substituting a daybed and a reproduction of Maxfield Parrish's "Daybreak"—a well-known Neoromantic painting in which, before a background of craggy mountains tinged with the first gold of dawn, a girl lies on her back on a Grecian porch with columns, at the very instant of being awakened by a bending adolescent—it is impossible to tell the sex, because of the position of the hands on the knees—who is entirely unclothed. It was Belle-Maman herself who chose this print from the art department of Ramspecks Downtown, perhaps because she imagined the reclining maiden in the tunic as herself and the metallic-hued bending child as me.

When I tired of studying this work of art—and in spite of its classic simplicity there were details that one discovered only after a tenth or a twentieth examination—I could always steal downstairs to the library, which could be reached by skirting around the sounds of revel coming from the dining room and the spacious Florentine salon, and find something to take upstairs to read. The library, a room decorated in gold and illuminated with heavy bronze lamps in the shape of caryatids, was well equipped and even impressive for a private collection. Many of the volumes were textbooks from Belle-Maman's days at Bennington, and others were books she had collected now and then on her shopping expeditions or received as selections from clubs—she belonged only to the better book clubs, those that specialized in reprints of classics in expensive bindings, or current books tending toward the avant-garde and the curious. I began where the books began, simply because they were arranged that way on the shelves—first Shakespeare and the Elizabethans, then Thomas Browne, Burton's *Melancholoy* (that was a puzzling one), Chatterton, Keates, Coleridge, Ann Radcliffe, Monk Lewis, Mary Shelley, Landor, and Swinburne. In a short time I had become an avid solitary reader, a practice that left me even thinner and more wan than before, but gave me a body of information about the human soul and the ways of the world far beyond my years. It also developed my imagination, perhaps even to an unhealthy degree; but certainly as a child I lived a rich life of the mind, one of which Javier and even Belle-Maman, with all her superiority and her pretensions to culture, could have had no notion. For hours on end I sat propped in pillows on the daybed holding a book on my knees, a melancholy and moody little creature with a pinched face and a shock of dark hair (I could see myself in the Art-Deco mirror on the opposite wall) in the grip of a powerful and—I began to suspect—malevolent enchantment. In my rather hectic state of excitement I was scarcely able to distinguish fact from fancy; I lost myself totally in these constructs of the imagination which, through some technical necromancy, had been impressed so vividly onto these slick and finely compressed sheets of wood-pulp. I wept with Emma when Rudolphe was faithless, and with Anna Karenina I flung myself under the train. As René, in his Breton castle, I cast enigmatic stares at my virgin sister Amélie, and fell into suicidal gloom when she withdrew into a convent. I looked into Chapman's Homer, and drew my breath in dismay with the Trojans, "Gasing for counsell on the entrailes warme." Converted momentarily to an orangutan, I stuffed the corpse up the chimney in the Rue Morgue. Strange where empathy will lodge; I suppose I should have associated myself with M. Dupin. Some of my reading no doubt was beyond my grasp, precocious as I was; I made little sense of *Ulysses*, and *Finnegans Wake* I suspected was a huge joke perpetrated on the reader by a puckish author. *The Story of O*, stolen from Javier's nightstand, was perfectly comprehensible to me, but struck me as improbable and a little pointless. The same with Sade's *Justine*, in full morocco with embossed titles and gilded edges. (This was Belle-Maman's book.) If there had been illustrations—but there weren't, in these expensive volumes designed for the most refined of bibliophiles. However, there were in Javier's funny papers.

A prominent feature of the library was my stepfather's collection of vintage comics—a valuable investment, as I was later given to understand, although I was not sure this was why he had collected them. These trifles filled a large glass case at one end of the room, never locked since Javier frequently took away an item to read in bed before he went to sleep. They began in the primitive period with Happy Hooligan and Krazy Kat, and proceeded on through the Golden Age of the genre with the Katzenjammer Kids, Moon Mullins, Gasoline Alley, Tarzan of the Apes, and Harold Teen. Others, carefully tucked away in the back (no doubt because they were more valuable investments), were indecent parodies—the Captain, knocked cold in a virile state while pursuing a shipwrecked maiden with his pants off, is taken advantage of by Mamma, who hasn't had such an opportunity in years, or Tarzan, swinging into his bower prepared to be greeted with "Me Jane," finds it instead occupied by a muscular female ape and has to bend to her stronger will. It was in these travesties that I first acquired some accurate information about the anatomy of love, and I also noted for later reflection that the aggressors in all or most of them were women. At my tender age I couldn't decide whether this was the way the world really worked, or whether it represented a convention in pornographic comics, or simply reflected something in Javier's personal tastes. I brooded; but in the end I went back to *The Castle of Otranto*, which I preferred.

A frequent visitor to the house in those days when I was nine or ten was my cousin Blanche, a female child a little younger than myself, and who was "slow," to use Belle-Maman's charitable euphemism. In reality her mind never developed enough for her to speak, but in recompense she learned to go to the toilet by herself, to use a knife and fork, and to go about the world with a proud and aristocratic air of hauteur that suggested she was far above the mundane mob of humanity who incessantly communicated trivialities to one another through squeaks and grunts of the larynx. Her parents — I believe her father was a cousin on my mother's side — worked in the daytime and couldn't afford to have her cared for by professionals, so they often left her on their way to work and called for her again in the evening. As a matter of fact she was not the only child who was brought to the house to play with me in those days; the Ramspecks, having no children of their own, were fond of collecting nephews and other indigent small relatives. But Blanche is the one who impressed herself on my memory most vividly. She resembled me enough that she might have been my sister. Like me, she was pale and thin with dark hair, and she always wore white; I, when she came to visit, was dressed like a miniature little man in a black suit and a shirt with a Byronic collar. "Aren't they a charm, the two of them," said Belle-Maman. "Like the figures on a wedding cake." We conducted ourselves with proper decorum during the morning, sitting on two chairs reading books; or at least Blanche gravely turned the pages, glancing at me now and then to see how it was done. She was endlessly patient and never bored; the simplest amusement was enough to occupy her for hours. At noon Belle-Maman would prepare for us a lunch of graham crackers and milk, and then she customarily went off shopping, or on one of her charities, leaving us to play unattended in the house for the rest of the day.

Our favorite resort, in these long and lazy afternoons, was the solarium at the rear of the house, a large high-ceilinged room with a terrazzo floor and a wall filled entirely with windows. When we pushed open the door from the salon the contrast to the rest of the house was enough to give a little frisson; we entered into a profuse and unkempt jungle, a landscape of Henri Rousseau. There were palm trees in wooden tubs, dwarf citruses (the odor of orange blossoms was one of several that pervaded the place), and magnolias with large icy-white blooms. Ivies and creepers worked their sticky tentacles along the glass, seeking toward the thin sunshine that fell onto this north side of the house. Immense Florentine terracotta vases stood about with nymphs and shepherds pursuing one another in friezes around their rims, and planter-pots hung on long wires from the ceiling, filled with drooping succulents and turning slowly in the slight stir of air that moved through the place. The atmosphere was warm and humid. In the silence there was a very faint rustling or crepitation, perhaps made in some way by the plants in their growing, and there were the other small sounds common to all deserted houses: the creaks and sighs of sunwarmed glass, the click of insects, unidentified and almost inaudible murmurs that came perhaps from a distant refrigerator or from the electrical wires buried in the walls. Although the plants crowded the room almost to bursting, there were open spaces here and there in the jungle, clearings large enough that Blanche and I could use them as enchanted make-believe bowers for our play.

Blanche was my first friend and, I might say, my first lover, not counting Belle-Maman. (Whom she complemented perfectly as a sentimental partner; Belle-Maman was always talking, and patted me you know where, whereas Blanche said nothing at all and conducted herself with impeccable chastity.) To while away our long afternoons in the solarium we played games: "Irish Castle," "Sleeping Beauty," or "Julio and Romanette in the Tomb." It was I who named them, of course, and I took the leading parts. The Sleeping Beauty was awakened with a kiss, and the point of Julio and Romanette was that its characters, thinly disguised facsimiles of my stepparents, lay dead and did nothing at all. In "Daybreak," imitated from the painting of Parrish, Blanche lay down in her white dress, and I took off my clothes and bent over her with my hands on my knees. Nothing happened; we smiled, I reclothed, she got up. I'd rather not discuss Irish Castle. Blanche was perfectly docile, understanding my instructions after only a little iteration and drill, and played her roles always with a sweet and dreamy smile suggesting that she was elsewhere but glad to lend her ghost insofar as it would serve my purposes. These idyllic pageants, with variations, continued until the horn of the dingy Plymouth owned by Blanche's parents was heard in the driveway, and our games came to an end. We never got caught at this, but we deserved to. Mr. Grimespan came upon us once, but only commented with his usual tolerance, "Kids will be little perverts."

To be fair, I ought to admit that as I grew older my stepfather made certain overtures toward a father-son relationship as this is popularly understood, in child-rearing books perhaps or in the funny papers. For instance, on one occasion (I must have been about ten) he somehow procured a baseball as hard as iron and an adult catcher's mitt in which my small hand wandered like a mouse in an overcoat, and invited me out on the lawn for a game of catch. "Knowing how to throw a ball is part of being a man," he told me. "I saw you heaving a sock at the laundry hamper the other day, and you had your elbow stuck out like a girl."

I stood at one end of the lawn and he at the other, and he took off the jacket of his three-piece worsted suit, folded it carefully, and set it on the grass. He was already perspiring and his beefy face was set in a grimace of determination. Then he wound up with elaborate curlicues and fired the thing at me. We never did find out whether I could throw it or not. His first pitch sizzled through the air past my ear and I never even saw it. When the second came, I was more alert and stuck up my sticklike little arm with the oversized mitt on the end of it. There was a sharp pain in my elbow, and the mitt and the ball flew away at different angles.

"Never mind the mitt," he told me.

When the third pitch came I was concerned only to save myself, but at this I was unsuccessful. The obdurate sphere struck me on the left clavicle, knocking me flat and inflicting a "green stick fracture," as the doctors at Childrens Hospital poetically termed it. It wasn't serious and didn't even need to be put in a cast. It just hurt like hell for six weeks or more.

"A tough guy," Javier ragged me. "You can dish it out but you can't take it."

Belle-Maman only raised an eyebrow, which she did skillfully and with eloquence. Being supercilious was part of the curriculum at Bennington. It is possible she had her own opinions of athletics, and even of Javier, but if so she never confided them to me.

After that his efforts at camaraderie were confined to chummy conversations. At mealtimes he kept firing remarks at me with a certain avuncular joviality, advising me that one should eat oysters (I would as soon have eaten slugs from the garden) because they "put lead in your pencil" and asking me what I found to talk about with my deaf-and-dumb girlfriend. "Let's feel that pitching arm" he would propose, clenching the broomstick inside my sleeve with his meaty fingers. He suggested that when summer came I might like to "work in women's underwear" at the store downtown, and offered me consolation when I developed a minor infection that had to be treated (back to Childrens Hospital) with a urethral catheter: "That's what's wrong with the world. Everyone's robbing Peter to pay Paul, and Peter gets sore, and everybody knows you can't do anything with a sore Peter." He had discovered that children could be fun. Fun for him, it goes without saying; not fun for me. Among his other levities, he always referred to my deceased bioparents as "the strolling players" and once when the frail and pale visage of Mae Meadows appeared unexpectedly on the TV screen (it was the Late Night Show, they didn't care what time I went to bed) he exclaimed, "Oh Gosh. It's the phthistic phantom. Everybody get out their handkerchiefs."

Two things can be discerned already in this account: first that I possessed an impressive power over women at an early age, having driven two of them to the point of violent folly, and successfully enthralled another into carrying out my odd and somewhat obscure will; and second that, except for these amorous proclivities, I was a creature who lived largely in the world of my private imagination. (Later when I encountered the expression "solitary vice" I thought it referred to reading.) I would have been blissfully content in my life with Belle-Maman—and with Blanche, the other part so to speak of the twinned female presence my dream-nature sought for—if this "family romance," as the Viennese sage so aptly puts it, had not been blighted by the intrusion into it of the hypotenuse of the triangle. But Javier I was not able to subdue, with all my charms. In the face of his blunt and hirsute tribal bullying, I could only take refuge in the traditional recourse of the artist faced with naked tyranny, satire; and in my case in its weakest form, the one consoling only to the artist himself, unpublished satire. Taking my models from the thousand books I had already read at my young age, I became a secret author, and illustrated my own works. At first my tales, penciled with care and with meticulous calligraphy into a lined school notebook, were mere imitations of my favorites: Chateaubriand, Mary Shelley, *The Castle of Otranto*, Mrs. Radcliffe, *Ligeia*. Occasionally there were excursions into verse. One of these efforts has been preserved in some way (I found it recently tucked into the lining of an old suitcase) and shows a precocious if somewhat imitative talent:

"Ah Blanche! thou Child of silence and Slow Time,
Could I but make thee immortal in my Rhyme,
Thy muted voice in Song might then persuade
My FRANCES dear to draw you to her breast,
Where then we three might dwell among the Blest."

The Keatsian pastiche of the first line I was unconscious of; the flaw in form (a quatrain-sandwich with an indigestible middle, or a ruba'i with a fifth line) I put down to originality. How a muted voice could persuade anything I didn't stop to ask myself. There was genuine feeling, and there was a certain bronzed clangor to the diction. I think that is enough for a child of eleven. But I seem to have wandered, in my fascination with this piece of orotund juvenalia. I was speaking of satire, and of the form of prose narrative.

As I have said, my earlier efforts at fiction were more or less frankly borrowed from the Gothic school of the previous century. But in time, and with practice, I began to develop a more original vein—more modern, with a post-psychoanalytic pertinence denied to our naive forefathers, and more expressive of my own personal drama and fate. Its frequently bizarre episodes took place in a Montenegrin landscape where it was always night, with a pitiless moon glowing on the black mountains. Its accoutrements were tombs, romantic chasms, gallows at crossroads, monasteries with thick walls to muffle shrieks, and ancient solitary pines. There were marble cliffs in the distance, in the manner of Jünger. And isolated chateaux. In this setting there took place suggestive dramas that I hardly understood myself, the murky but clairvoyant insights of a boy who knew nothing about the world but, in a dark corner tucked away in the bottom of his mind, guessed all. My male characters behaved at times like the half-deranged and moody heroes of Gothic novels, at other times like pornographic Tarzans. The heroines were divided into two classes; immature damsels in peril, pale from confinement in castles and yet curiously complacent and knowing; and broad-breasted matrons in classic gowns who in some way beamed electric rays at the male characters from their all-seeing eyes, causing them to fall into trances in which they carried out complicated slaveries according to direction. "O Dame Regina," one of these marble-browed heroes cried to his dominatrix, "under thy powerful gaze the marrow of my bones turns to water, and I am helpless in the thrall of thy feminine will." "Go then," she intoned, "and seek out the maiden Ysrafel and declare thy love to her, which is only my own love disguised in manly raiments, and acting through thee my minion." He (his name was Lord Garth) eventually after some searching found Israfel in an isolated castle, but when he made his declaration, she only gave a shriek and turned to vapor. When Garth went back to Regina, he found that she too had vanished and left behind her only a set of leg-irons in a dungeon, which magically closed about his ankles as soon as he applied them. And there his skeleton was found, some generations later, by wandering shepherds seeking shelter for the night.

In an attempt to imitate the engravings found in the books I borrowed from the library, I often experimented with making my own illustrations. For this I used India ink, an old-fashioned pen with a steel nib, and the best drawing paper, a medium which had the disadvantage of being uncorrectable but was well suited to simulate the nocturnal black-and-white effects of the originals. Bent over my worktable, my fingers inky and little freckles of black spotting my face, I passed hours at limning old castles, sinuous rills, and rather frayed-looking heroes and heroines on the white paper as spotted and soiled as myself. Naturally I had no training in drawing, and I found that a vivid imagination was no help in a craft demanding so much technical expertise; the results were often disappointing. Craggy characters like Lord Garth came out fairly well, but feminine beauty was beyond my skill. It was clear that I would never be an artist, and I had no ambition to be. Still, pasted into the schoolboy notebooks along with the prose, these illustrations provided some sort of locus for the organ of vision to fix upon as the mind made its way through the story. Taking the texts along with the pictures, the total effect was at least comparable to that of the genuine novels from the library. The black-and-white speckled covers of the notebooks, while far from the full morocco with gilt, lent an old-fashioned and Victorian tone not without its own kind of elegance. I was pleased with my efforts, accepting it as axiomatic that they were intended only for an audience of one, myself. And indeed who else could I have shown them to? Blanche, my only friend, might have smiled in her sweet way at the pictures but the text was inaccessible to her. And Belle-Maman, I felt, would only have made some ironic witticism over these productions that were distinguished, on the one hand, by their technical ineptitude, and on the other by the embarrassing insight they offered into my most private mental processes. As for Javier—at the thought I thrust the notebooks away into the drawer and carefully locked it, hiding the key under my pillow.

So matters went on until one day I was freed from the limitations of this crude and imitative representation by the unexpected influence of disease. In consequence of a touch of intestinal flu, I was confined, theoretically to my bed but in practice to my room; after everyone had left the house I resumed my place at the worktable with my pen and India ink. Belle-Maman, before floating out of the house in a silk dress and a picture hat, had administered to me a few drops of paregoric, which as everyone knows is a camphorated tincture of opium, perfectly harmless and suited for treating children for such ailments as colic and flux of the bowels. I was still feverish, and my overheated imagination was no doubt further stimulated by the influence of the magical poppy-wine. As though in a trance I moved the pen across the paper, hardly knowing where the images came from and watching with curiosity as they flowed from the scratchy tip of the pen. The fever and the drug together had broken through the membrane to the subconscious and liberated a creative power whose existence I had never before guessed. What emerged, as I watched in fascination, was a Krazy Kat landscape decorated, not with castles and tombs, but with brickyards, jails, sterile mountains, and white crescent-moons in black skies. The characters were all animalistic. A small and shy white mouse, who had nothing to do with Ignatz and his brick, was a dream-version of the maiden in peril of the Gothic romances. There was also a wasp-waisted hymenopter with a narrow derrière, wearing her hat at a tilt and swaying her hip with one hand, and a bulky ovine patriarch with a wooly face who managed with some difficulty to stand upright on his teetery hooves. Dipping my pen impatiently into the bottle, I covered sheet after sheet with scenes from this nocturnal world with its bizarre inhabitants. In some of them the Sheep was preparing to kick the Ant in the rear, and in return was about to be clubbed by a muscular gorilla named Adelbert—no doubt influenced by the orangutan in *Murders in the Rue Morgue*, but also a thinly disguised persona of the artist himself. In the background a timid Blanche-Mouse watched with bright eyes to see how it would all come out. I eventually abandoned all other scenes to concentrate on this one, and I added details from draft to draft. In the final version, I depicted the ovine tyrant in an impressive state of manliness imitated from Tarzan and the Katzenjammer Captain, complete with glowing tip. Art copies Art—of course I had no knowledge of such a phenomenon from the real world.

By this time I was breathing hard, and no doubt the whole business wasn't doing my fever any good. I contemplated my creation and thought for a moment. Something was lacking. It was that this drawing, unlike my previous ones, was not an illustration for a written text but only a piece of graphic art in isolation; there were no words to go with the images. I thought of reversing the process and writing a novel to illustrate the picture, so to speak, although of course I would have had to make several more drawings. But then it occurred to me that I had ignored the traditional form of verbalization common to the cartoon form itself. Taking up my pen again, I drew a line from the Ant's mouth, and above it an oblong like a fat dirigible. I did the same for the Sheep, except that his balloon was larger to correspond to his greater bulk. Then, driven by some imp of the perverse, I filled in these outlines with the appropriate utterances. Cried Ant: "Oh Ramspecker, what is this blessing I see so boldly blooming and tumefying?" And he to her: "It is not for you, Ant-Fanny, it is destined for others, so go off and palpate your poppet's piccolo as usual." Adelbert was saying nothing at all; he was about to fell the sheepish bully with his bludgeon, which substituted in him both for words and for a visible phallus—that part of him was decorously hidden in fur that covered him from head to feet, like the raccoon coat of a football fan.

Still a little giddy, and with the world buzzing pleasantly around me, I locked this production away in the drawer with the notebooks. And there it remained until a fateful day when—well, let me back up. What I am telling you, of course, is not only an account of the facts that happened but also a story. We all live stories, whether we realize it or not. And in a story, there is only one ending to an incident in which a child draws or writes something which is only for his own most private use, and which he wishes above all to conceal from his parents. What else could happen but that his secrets should be cruelly bared to the very eyes they were intended to be hidden from ? For what else, in fact, has he hidden them?

It was perhaps a week later, while I was still convalescing from my illness, that the Ramspecker (excuse me, Javier) came rampaging into my room and flinging my possessions around in search of his copy of *The Story of O*. Having a basically criminal mind himself, he was quickly able to guess where I had hidden the key. In the drawer he found not only his book but also the cartoon, which he flourished in triumphant indignation before the eyes of Belle-Maman. She sighed, and I was summoned to be judged. "What's this filth?" he demanded, holding it up and snapping his teeth at me. "My God! what have I been nourishing in my bosom—at my expense—a serpent—an artist!"

Belle-Maman only remarked that it was not very well drawn, a critique which cut far deeper than Javier's pretense of outraged rectitude.

"I won't raise my hand against a sick child," he bellowed on, "but so help me, if I find you up to such tricks again, I'll smack your little—"

"Javier," interjected Belle-Maman hastily. Then she murmured distractedly, unaware no doubt of the chain of association that had connected in her own mind, "My dear little Popo . . ."

She had not used this endearment for years. And the sound of the childish bisyllable, half forgotten and coming to me now like a talisman out of the remote shadows of my infancy, clarified for me in a single instant, like the abrupt jelling of a crystalline solution, the enigma of my own identity and vocation. I was an artist, yes! and I knew now that my fate was to follow in the footsteps of the poet-namesake whose image had lain concealed—in all those years since my babyish fingers had first strayed upon his Book—in the obscure and viscous folds of my memory. Obeying Ramspecker's stern injunction, and taking account as well of Belle-Maman's opinion of my drawing skill, I never again tried my hand at illustrating my own fictions. The stories I write now are well capable of evoking their own bizarre mental pictures through the sheer power of my skill in language, as the reader of these lines can see. It goes without saying that I have made a specialty of the Gothic, and in time I have become quite adept at it. Not enough to make a living, of course, very few do, but I have been able to supplement my meager royalties and sustain myself by working part time in Griswold's Slumber Chapel. In doing so—in every step and detail of a life which has become a work of art—I honor the memory of that mysterious Avatar who bequeathed to me, not only his talent, but his taste and delicacy in matters aesthetic.

THE LINGUIST

It was several months after my arrival in Cathay, I believe, that I first heard of the odd sexual arrangements in Cipangu; or, if I had heard of the matter earlier, it for some reason failed to catch my attention. The first reference to it that I remember, in fact, came in the form of a joke. I was at a party, I forget now exactly where, and someone told a young man who was a little effeminate, or was pretending to, "Oh, go to Cipangu." Half in fun and half in exasperation.

I inquired further. At first my questioning produced only laughter, but finally they calmed down and told me solemnly that in Cipangu there were three sexes. I studied them. Were they pulling my leg? No, it seemed to be perfectly serious. Although they quickly changed the subject.

It *was* a joke perhaps—a national slur—just as we in the West sometimes refer to men who like boys as Bulgarians. But the more I questioned the less I found out. It was as though there were some sort of taboo, not against discussing the subject, but against discussing it seriously. As a matter of fact no one in Cathay knew very much about it. None of them had ever been to Cipangu, since travel there was forbidden—

by the Cathayans themselves, I gathered, and not by the Cipanguti. I again evoked laughter when I asked what would happen to me if I went there. Was this because the citizens there played trios instead of duets? No one would tell me.

Naturally I was intrigued, and my curiosity was only sharpened by the prohibition on travel to this odd country. And I soon found out that, like most laws, this one too could be circumvented. I found out whom to pay. It was not very much. And with only a handbag, since I didn't intend to stay very long, I embarked in a small sailing vessel for Cipangu, a few days' sail to the east across the inland sea. Since the prevailing winds were from the west, the voyage went quickly. I wasn't an expert on navigation and it didn't occur to me to wonder how we were going to get back. I found out, when the time came for me to return to Cathay; there were slaves under the deck who worked pedals, turning a helix under water which propelled the ship at the pace of a walking man. Perhaps for this reason, the fare for the return voyage was quadrupled. I hadn't counted on this, and so I myself labored at those pedals for thirteen days. But that is another story.

The kingdom of Cipangu consists of a cluster of islands, four large ones and a number of smaller ones, about a hundred and fifty leagues to the east of Cathay, and curled like a scorpion so that the sea between the two countries is enclosed and protected. From the port where I landed, it was another day and a half in a sedan chair to Kyo-tu, the capital city. But even before I set out on the trip, simply gazing out from my ship at the people on the dockside, I was able to see that there was something very odd indeed about the population of Cipangu.

It was some time before I myself was able to sort out this complicated matter and make sense out of it. And information was hard to come by: just as the Cathayans are humorists about matters of the bodily functions, so the Cipanguti are sentimentalists, and this makes it equally hard to get a straight story out of them. But what it came to, as I gradually pieced it together, is that there were indeed three sexes in Cipagnu, all necessary for the act of procreation: or simply for what is called amour in other lands, leaving procreation out of it. This state of matters resulted, as far as I could determine, from an evolution of the human type taking place over many centuries, and it appears that the Cipanguti began by modifying—perhaps in an attempt to extirpate them—the few homosexuals who appeared more or less naturally in their population. Whether these were male or female homosexuals I was not able to find out, and indeed the terms male and female are of very little use in describing the sexual arrangements of the Cipanguti. Instead they consist of three types.

1. The *ran-ja*, plural *ran-ji*. This word signifies more or less "the lover." The *ran-ja* is beardless, but virile. He is the one who carries the short sharp sword called the *han-dzi*. The type is slightly smaller than the average of the population, but hard and athletic. The typical *ran-ja* remains lithe, unwrinkled, and attractive into old age. My first impression of Cipangu was of the extraordinary numbers of these acrobatic young eunuchs—as they appeared to me—strolling haughtily about the streets with their hands on the pommels of the *han-dzis* at their sides.

2. The *tan-go*, plural *tan-ghi*, "the beloved." This sort of person has short hair and fine features, somewhat wider hips than a *ran-ja*, and a sweet and passive temperament. A small mouth with slightly pouting lips is admired, and cultivated. The *tan-ghi* whiten their faces with rice powder, and have contralto voices.

3. The *ban-go*, plural *ban-ghi*. The word is difficult to translate: it is variously rendered as parent, guardian, nurturer, or child-rearer. The members of this gender perform some functions of both mother and father. The *ban-go* has facial hair from birth; persons of this sort are born with a beard but have no pubic hair at any age. The typical *ban-go* looks mature even as a child, where the *ran-ja* looks youthful even in old age.

I was unaware of all these nuances when I attempted to disembark from my ship, but I did find out that the Cipanguti are so jealous of the purity of this arrangement, and so fearful of reverting to the antique and almost forgotten bisexuality, which they regard as an animal barbarism, that by law every male foreigner who wishes to visit their land must first have his genital parts cut off with their razor-sharp *han-dzis*—or, if female, be stitched permanently neuter. This was the source of the jokes of my friends in Cathay. This discovery made me very fearful, but nevertheless I was determined to stay in Cipangu and find out more about their extraordinary customs. I therefore argued to the immigration police, successfully, that the law was intended to apply to foreigners, that is Cathayans, and that I was not a foreigner but a Venetian, which was quite another thing, a man from the moon. I also claimed that I was impotent, which was not true, but I did not expect to have any opportunity to demonstrate the contrary.

At that point, of course, I had no notion of what I was getting into. Off I went in my sedan chair, and was soon installed in comfortable lodgings in the capital. In the succeeding weeks I managed to piece together a good deal of information about this peculiar and intriguing aspect of Cipangu culture. The Cipanguti are not very hospitable in their homes, but they lead an active public life. Much of their time is spent in tea-rooms, cafés, restaurants, and other public places, or simply strolling on the avenues of the capital lined with beautifully landscaped gardens. So, although it was a while before I formed any personal attachments or was invited to anyone's home, I was able to observe a good deal on the subject of love among the Cipanguti, at least in its more public aspects.

Trisexuality is a good deal more complex than one might at first imagine, at least for a person like me who does not have a mathematical mind and is not adept at the subject of permutations. Still the implications are fairly obvious. Assuming three genders, it is clear that a 1 and a 2, after falling in love (and romantic love is much esteemed and practiced in Cipangu), must search about the world for a 3 with whom they can both fall in love, and this is not easy. It might be imagined that it is the *ran-ja* and *tan-go*, the Lover and Beloved, who normally fall in love first and then go in search of a Nurturer, but this is not necessarily the case. The three sexes may fall in love in any combination. As you can imagine, this enormously increases the probablility of tragic or unrequited love, and indeed Cipangu literature is mainly pathetic and devoted to the various ways in which love can go wrong. It also inhibits the birth rate, which bothers no one, since Cipangu is a small country and the population already almost fills it.

Many times in public places in the capital I saw couples, consisting of combinations of any two of the three types, fondling each other or walking arm in arm; there is no disapproval of public affection and in fact it is encouraged as a form of sex education. (The manuals we have on such subjects, the clandestine pornographic magazines, the teaching of sexual techniques in the schools, would horrify and disgust the Cipanguti, since they would be thought of as unromantic.)

Such couples always had a melancholy and furtive look about them, a look of seeking something in the distance, since they were both on the lookout for a 3. Yet they both knew that the chances of their finding a 3 with whom they would both fall in love were miniscule; thus their melancholy and lovelorn mein. More than likely, 1 would find a 3 who was not attractive to 2; or 1 and 2 would find a 3 with whom they both fell in love, only to find that 3 was attracted to 2 but not to 1. Thus the possibilities for unrequited love were enormous, in fact mathematically infinite.

Yet, as in other lands, love often found a way. Occasionally one would see in public places a completed couple, which of course was more properly called a trio. The three—Lover, Beloved, and Nurturer—would walk together with their arms intricately enlaced, or sit in a café caressing one another according to a system I was never quite able to grasp, since it required each person to do two things at once, and there were three persons involved.

As for the actual act of sexual intercourse, I was never able to find out anything at all specific about it, since the Cipanguti with their cult of romanticism and their highly literary or even sentimental attitude toward love prefer to draw a veil of absolute privacy over the subject. What I did learn, or conjecture, came partly from my observations of public caressing, since I could not but conclude that these gestures had some relation to the ultimate erotic act. But even more rewarding was my sudden insight, at a certain point in my visit to Cipangu, that the dance in all countries is a kind of analogue of the sexual act as it is regarded in that culture, except that in most cases the procedure is translated from the horizontal to the vertical for symbolic purposes. (Witness the flamenco, and the Viennese waltz: the first implying a sexual tradition of rigid puritanism and repression which breaks out in foot-stamping and fire, and the second suggesting a thorough-going decadence combined with a spurious and hypocritical romanticism). These analogies suggested that, first of all the Cipanguti when making love lay coiled in a ring like three snakes; that their caresses were ambivalent, that is that each partner simultaneously caressed the two others; and that the sexual parts and sexual functions of the three did not correspond in any way to the division of the sexes as we are familiar with them; for instance it was not the case, as we might suppose, that the Lover and Beloved corresponded to male and female in our culture, and the Nurturer was a kind of added or superfluous partner. The *ran-ja* was only in some senses a pseudo-male; he carried the sharp *han-dzi* but he was beardless and had a high, sweet, and somewhat feminine voice. You will notice that I fall into the trap of using a masculine pronoun for the *ran-ja*, simply because I am restricted to the resources of my own language. But in Cipanguti there are three sets of pronouns: three nominatives, *ro*, *to*, and *bo*; three accusatives, *r'an*, *t'an*, and *b'an*; and three possessives, *j'mein*, *j'sein*, and *j'dein*. So I should properly say of the *ran-ja* that *ro* was beardless and that *j'mein* voice was soprano; but this will complicate matters too much.

In the same way, the *tan-go* was female only in some qualities, while the *ban-go* partook of male and female characteristics in varying aspects and certain degrees. (The average *ban-go*, of whatever age, looked something like a middle-aged woman with a beard; yet some were remarkably attractive. One of the disorienting sensations of visiting Cipangu was that one could suddenly imagine being sexually attracted to a middle-aged woman with a beard.)

Another tentative conclusion I arrived at was little more than a hypothesis, since I had no practical evidence, other than certain cryptic references in romantic literature, to support it. This was that two separate acts of coitus are necessary for procreation. In the first, which is more or less preliminary, the seed is transferred from the *ran-ja* to the womb of the *tan-go*, or to some convex receptacle in her person. There the embryo grows more or less in the manner familiar to us, until the time of a subsequent coitus which is more important and more complex. In this act, the tiny embryo is somehow translated from the conception-sac of the *tan-go* to the much more capacious womb of the *ban-go*, while simultaneously the *ran-ja* implants a new seed into the now vacant conception-sac. It might be imagined that this production-line would produce an awful lot of babies, if that is what they are called in Cipanguti; no one ever talks about them and they are not referred to in literature. But the fact is that the mathematical obstacles against happy triangular love are so great that this event, or double event, only rarely takes place. When it does, one can tell by the radiant faces of the trio when they appear in public. And the event is celebrated in literature—in fact it invariably forms the climax of every story and poem—where it is called the *piru-dzi*, a term borrowed from astronomy which means the conjunction of three stars at a single point. To hear, or more properly read in a story, that a trio had three-starred always seemed to me faintly humorous, suggesting the classification of European hotels; but I had to admit that the kiss, which plays so large a part in the climactic scenes of our own literature, is also a somewhat comic act, since such a labial contact has no more biological function than the nose-rubbing of Eskimos, and is even a little disgusting. (I had a Venetian friend once who would kiss his mistress, or even allow her to kiss the most intimate part of him, but would not drink from a water-glass after her lips had touched it.)

I have said there was no pornography in Cipangu, since

the sentimentality of the Cipanguti would have prevented them from taking an interest in these crasser aspects of the subject. Yet there was something analogous to it, which was called *pez-pech* or Forbidden Word. This was a literature, consisting of poorly-printed pamphlets on bad paper, sold by the double-widowed *ban-ghi* who begged in the marketplace, and dealing with the various forms of adultery or betrayal of the vows of triple matrimony. This whole subject, as one can imagine, was unbelievably complex. It can be seen immediately that for a *tan-go*, for example, to betray her *ran-ja* and *bango* to any effect, it was necessary for her to find simultaneously another *ran-ja* and *ban-go* who were attracted to her, and who might be parts of the same matrimony or persons who didn't even know each other—in which case it was necessary for them too to fall in love. Thus, if we drive the possibilities to the mathematical absolute, we can imagine members of the same matrimony simultaneously having affairs with six other persons, thus causing the betrayal of eight separate individuals, including their own partners, at the miniumum: or, if we suppose that the adulterous lovers chosen are none of them members of the same matrimony, fourteen—I believe my calculations are correct. Whether this sort of thing actually ever took place I wasn't able to ascertain; yet I still have a number of soiled and shoddy *pez-pech* pamphlets to prove that the Cipanguti at least envisioned such possibilities.

I did, however, finally succeed in having sexual relations while I was in Cipangu, in spite of my promises to the immigration police. I am sorry, however, that I can't tell very much about the circumstances, since the persons involved, who numbered either two or three, got me so drunk with sweet wine first, in order to conceal their secrets, that I scarcely knew what I was doing. I remember only an extraordinary number of naked bodies laced together, and also the sense of an excruciating pleasure that I felt, a sensation that persisted in me for days afterwards as a kind of reverse premonition of paradise, a sweet aching in the bones that left no doubt that something important had happened to me. Whether the two or three Cipanguti involved in this incident enjoyed it too I have no idea. I think it is more probable that they committed this highly illicit act not out of passion but in a kind of reckless and jesting defiance of the authorities. This sort of behavior is common enough in youth in all cultures; and I have no doubt that if more foreigners were admitted to Cipangu it would happen more often, so that the authorities were right in being suspicious of my desire to enter the country, and would have done better to cut off my private parts with a *han-dzi*. Because it seems to me very possible that only a little bisexuality, if introduced, might spread like wildfire and destroy the Cipanguti uniqueness of physiology; and who can say whether life is more pleasant in our own culture or in this remote land where relations between persons are interlaced with the most complex kind of melancholy and sentiment, and where people are so busy with their personal problems that they have no time for war, politics, or crimes of gain such as robbery or embezzlement. (The government of Cipangu is rudimentary and consists mainly of the immigration police, who also bury the dead and arrest an occasional *ban-go* for selling *pez-pech* pamphlets.)

But let me tell how this happened. I imagine everyone is panting to know. I met Rezato and Tam'ya in a café. (I should have explained earlier that all *ran-ji* have names beginning in R, all *tan-go* with T, and all *ban-go* with B, so that as soon as you meet somebody you are in no doubt about his sex.) The cafés in the capital are very pleasant places and I formed the habit of spending a good deal of time in them. They are usually set in gardens, with flowering trees and carp-ponds, and in summer the walls are removed so that there is a feeling of being indoors and outdoors at once, and a cool breeze passes through bringing the odor of flowers. Coffee, tea, wine, and tiny sweet cakes are served. The particular wine of Cipangu is called *shan-pen* and is made from Hibiscus and Magnolia blossoms, so that it is sweet and tastes more like perfume than like wine; yet it is possible to drink an awful lot of it. It is lightly carbonated; the Cipanguti say "it has stars in it," a very sexy thought.

In general, it is easy to meet people in cafés: there is a good deal of talking and arch glancing from table to table, and since the tables are low and you sit on the floor on lambskin cushions, there is always room for one more to join the party. Yet any acquaintances you make in a café are confined to the café; you may think you are a good friend of a person you have met in a café, until you find that he will not even recognize you when he passes you in the street. In fact, if you meet a person in a café and then happen to encounter him in another café, he still may pretend not to recognize you. It is necessary for you to become his friend in *that* café too. You will see what I mean when I say that personal relations in Cipangu are terribly complicated. In any case, an implication of all this is that, even though you become quite intimate with a café friend, there is no question of being invited to his home or meeting the other members of his family trio, assuming that he is married. As for couples who are going around to cafés in the hope of meeting a third party, they are sacrosanct; unless, of course, they fall in love with you across the room, and you with them. In the case of foreigners, of course—well, there are so few foreigners in Cipangu that no rules exist.

This made my encounter with Rezato and Tam'ya all the more remarkable. There I sat, or squatted in a kind of lotus position on my cushion, and they were making unmistakable eyes at me from the next table. Rezato was an extremely attractive person. He was small, even his arms and legs were small, but they gave the impression of being as tough as wrought-iron. He had a smooth and fair beardless face, the face of an adolescent in our culture, but his glance was steely and assured. His hair was long, Tam'ya's was short. She (once again, pardon my inadequate pronouns) seemed a little older, but this was probably only on account of her broad hips and deeper voice. She gave somehow the impression of a large placid doll; perhaps it was the face whitened with rice-powder, and the pouting mouth which was cultivated by *tan-ghi* from the time of childhood. In her case there was a slightly ironic quality to the lips, a little tightening or crease at the corners of the mouth, that I had not noticed in other *tan-ghi.* She was clad in a short wrap-around robe that came only halfway to her knees and showed her fine white legs to advantage. Both of them, I now saw, were examining me with interest, Rezato with a steely and cool, unsmiling intensity, Tam'ya with obvious coyness.

Naturally they knew who I was. To my knowledge, I was the only foreigner in the capital at that time. It is always flattering to be the object of concupiscence, yet I was a little confused, not to say disturbed. What did they want of me? Their own two sexes were obvious. I had never thought of myself as a Nurturer and that is not the sex I would have picked for myself if I had been a Cipanguti. But my intuition soon told me that they did not regard me as a *ban-go* either. They were intrigued with me precisely because I was not a member of any of the three sexes, and yet I was a young and attractive person. It was exactly as though a person of some Cipanguti sex, say a *ran-ja*, were transported to some city in the West. He would seem a warrior, yet a child, yet a woman;

and to persons whose tastes were a little peculiar, or who were bored with the conventional arrangements, this might be highly attractive. Rezato and Tam'ya were not normal to their culture; I don't mean to say that they were perverse, but simply that they were slightly bored with their lives and vulnerable to devious impulses. And I have to confess that I found them attractive too. After all, I recognized for the first time, I was not an average representative of my own culture either. First of all, I had left the West of my own volition and come to this remote part of the world, and second, as soon as I heard about the odd goings-on in Cipangu I set hastily off for the place under the impulse of a powerful curiosity. I began to get a little clearer insight now into my motives. Rezato and Tam'ya were attractive to me — not only both of them, but both of them at once — there was no question now about that.

Would they come to my table or I go to theirs? In the end it was I who moved, and folded my legs onto the cushion across the table from them, while not one muscle changed in the expressions of their faces. Rezato continued to study me with a steely intensity, and Tam'ya maintained her doll-like irony.

"I'm Polo," I told them.

"Yes, we know."

"Cipangu has very interesting customs," I began banally, partly because banality was the custom in the early stages of making an acquaintance, and partly because my knowledge of the language was still imperfect and I preferred to speak in simple sentences.

"What are you drinking? Ah! *shan-pen*. Waiter! another bottle of *shan-pen*."

Tam'ya was drinking wine too, and Rezato sipped at a cup of tea. The tea in Cipangu is made from dried Oleander leaves, is highly poisonous until it is filtered through potash, and has a delicate flavor of pine-sap. Just as we in the West say that wine provokes the desire and unprovokes the performance, so in Cipangu they say that Oleander-tea unprovokes the desire but provokes the performance. Rezato took his only a sip at a time. He asked me, "Which customs do you find particularly interesting?"

We were still following the conventional litany. "Those concerned with love," I told him.

"In what respect do you find the customs concerning love interesting?"

The *shan-pen* came and Rezato filled my glass. I had already had several glasses and was beginning to feel—starry, I suppose is the word. We went on talking about this and that. Working my way carefully through the slight alcoholic fuzz, I attempted to form a rather complicated sentence: "*Han-dzi diri porutu piru?*" Are you two part of a Three? This, I knew, was a question that was never asked; but perhaps anything might be permitted a foreigner.

Rezato countered, "I imagine there are many interesting customs in your country too."

"Yes. The arrangements regarding love, however, are a great deal simpler, so that we have time left for other things."

"What sort of things?" Rezato inquired politely.

"For example, we make machines that can kill people at a great distance."

"Ah Yes. Killing people in your country is permitted, as I have heard."

"Only under some circumstances."

"What circumstances?"

I was about to explain the circumstances were in time of war, and in the case of persons convicted of capital crimes; then I realized that there was no word for either war or crime in Cipanguti. Imitating Rezato's devious tact, I merely murmured,

"They are people that everyone agrees are bad."

"I don't see much point in killing people," said Rezato.

"Neither do I."

"Have you ever killed anyone?" asked Tam'ya, who seemed to take another sort of interest in the matter of homicide, an interest in *me* rather than in the question itself.

"No. Neither at a long distance nor at a short distance."

They encouraged me to drink more *shan-pen*. I was not sure any more whether I could stand up if I tried.

"Are you married?" Tam'ya asked me abruptly.

"No. However," I added, "in my country it is possible to commit the act of love without being married."

"Ah," said Rezato. There was a pause, and then Tam'ya asked, "Have you ever committed the act of love?"

"Yes."

Rezato sipped his tea—the potion that unprovokes desire, but provokes the performance. I was getting a little muddled as to what course of events this might imply.

"Now," said Rezato, "it is impossible for us to leave together, so Tam'ya and I will go, and you wait for only a minute and then follow us down the avenue."

Without another word they both got up and left. They were gone in an instant, before I had a chance to say anything. I was left sitting cross-legged at the table, looking across the room at a middle-aged *ran-ja* who was a known member of the immigration police. He was wearing the official headgear of his service, which looked something like a western top hat with the brim removed and a violet tassel on top. "Immigration police" is actually a rather bad translation; literally it is *Por-na-Pangu* or "Corps of National Sanctity." He stared back at me without any particular expression on his face.

Needless to say I got up, after exactly the prescribed minute, and followed Razato and Tam'ya down the avenue. They had their arms entwined about each other according to the usual custom, which slowed them down enough so that I was able to follow them without difficulty. They turned off the avenue into a lane that led through the gardens, and in five minutes we came to a small and attractive house no different from the other, with *fa'aa* or Climbing Orchids clinging along the eaves. The walls of the house could be opened like those of the café, and as soon as I was inside Rezato slid them shut. Tam'ya went away to repair her cosmetics, and Bo-dai entered the room. (Of course there *were* three of them, I am able to remember now, through the winey haze that surrounds the event). She seemed to know exactly what was up; she scarcely glanced at me, although she did so with a little smile, and she carried a tray with a bottle of *shan-pen* and three glasses on it. She looked like—how can I explain?—a portrait of one's mother in her girlhood, found by accident in an old album. Such discoveries produce the revelation that one's mother once was, and perhaps may still be, a sex-object. That Bo-dai was no longer young, and that she had a neat auburn beard, was of no consequence. As for the beard, it only gave her a spiritual and understanding look, something like that of the Redeemer as depicted in Western iconography. If you ask me what I thought I was doing in feeling amorous toward the Redeemer, I have no answer. I wasn't thinking at all. Probably it was the effect of the *shan-pen*.

I was made to drink more of this starry elixir, and raised no objection. Somehow my clothes came off and everyone gazed curiously at me. Someone murmured, "Barbaric." And another voice—yet softly, with a faint sensuous irony, "Like a dog." (For dogs, in Cipangu, are bisexual just as they are everywhere else). Rezato sipped his tea. He told the others, "Be sure the sliding walls are latched."

Yes, I was ready to be a dog! I panted, wagged my tail, and

prepared to lie down and roll over. How the four of us were translated from the vertical to the horizontal I have no clear recollection. I do remember that the floor, like the cushions in the café, was upholstered in lambskin. All I can say after that—I am sorry that I overdid the *shan-pen*, so that I can't give a more circumstantial account—is that for the next three-quarters of any hour I had the impression that I was enjoying the delights of four sexes at once, my own and their three. No one spoke, or only in pants and brief murmurs. In the middle of our delights there was a curious interruption. I heard the unmistakable sound of an infant wail from the next room, Bo-dai left our quartet which temporarily became a trio with no perceptible diminution in its activity, and after a few moments the wail turned to a coo. Bo-dai slipped back into the snake-ring and we went on. However, I was becoming a little alarmed. This was the sort of thing you could not engage in very often, I remember thinking, or you would explode, or break into three pieces. Another mathematical thought occurred to me, that four people have sixteen limbs. It seemed like more.

The next thing I remember (I have always hated phrases like that, in old-fashioned stories) is that, fully conscious but not quite aware of who was doing what, I was being carried out of the house and laid down in the garden of the house next door, across the hedge. My eyes were closed. Perhaps I slept for a while. It was summer and the air was mild. I was still naked but my clothes were laid beside me with my hand resting on them—perhaps to reassure me that they were still there. After a long time I heard a slight noise and opened my eyes. A few feet away an aged *ban-go* artist, complete with easel, was painting my portrait in water-colors. Of course there is no photography in Cipangu.

I put on my clothes and went back to my lodgings, imagining

that that was the end of the matter. And so it was, for a long time. It was early autumn when the landlord of my lodging-house told me that someone wished to speak with me. I came out into the open patio of the building and found that it was an official of the *Por-na-Pangu*, the same one who had stared at me when I left the café to follow my two friends. He required me to go with him to an unspecified place, for an unspecified purpose. Since I knew there was no crime in Cipangu and no jails, I had no apprehensions. We walked to the local *Por-na-pangu* office, then were put in sedan chairs and taken across the city. Following into a low and modest, but bureaucratic looking building after the officer, I found that there was perhaps no crime and no jails in Cipangu, but there were courts of law. Arraigned before a magistrate in a long skirt and a kind of violet tam-o-shanter (at first I was puzzled as to her sex, but she was an aged *ban-go*) were my three friends. I was invited to sit down on the cushion, and the others—Rezato, Tam'ya, and Bo-dai—remained standing. The officer then left the room; no one seemed concerned that I would take to my heels, or the others either. I was not allowed to speak, neither were the accused. There were no witnesses, there was no evidence, and there was no defense. That the crime in question had been committed was tacitly accepted by all, including the culprits. The magistrate too remained silent and seemed to be half-asleep. After a brief summary of the circumstances, read by a clerk, the bailiff pronounced the sentence. Rezato was banished to Ho-Kado, the northernmost island of the country, Tam'ya to another island in the west, and Bo-dai to the far south. They were never to see one another again and never to attempt any form of communication. As for me, I was to be conducted to the border and expelled. A modest sum was appropriated for my transportation by sedan chair.

It was a thoroughly sentimental punishment, typical of the country. I was a bit surprised at the reactions of my three friends. It was Rezato who wept, taking his hand for the first time from the pommel of his *han-dzi* to wipe the moisture from his eyes. Bo-dai repeated over and over again, "Pity, Sir Magistrate. Have pity." It was Tam'ya who was stoic. She gazed at the magistrate almost contemptuously, nothing about her showing any emotion, her rice-powder face and her ironic pout exactly the same.

None of the three met my glance. I wondered what they thought of me. The magistrate woke up, fussed around, and seemed to be looking for some paper or other. She ignored the three people still standing before her. They were slightly behind me, and I didn't turn my head. After a while I heard Bo-dai inquiring in a small plaintive voice, "But what about our *kokoru?*" And that was how I learned the Cipanguti word for baby.

THE ORPHAN BASSOONIST

In this unreal city, floating on the water and built out of improbable dreams and stone fantasies, I made the acquaintance of Professor Crispi. I believe it was on the vaporetto that I first encountered him. A nervous personage in an old-fashioned black coat a little too large for him, a complexion pink and splotchy like underdone veal even though veal of the highest quality, an expression simultaneously harassed and furtive. He resembled, perhaps, one of those anonymous Flemish sinners in the landscapes of Hieronymus Bosch who are afraid to look over their shoulders because they fear, correctly, that some unspeakable demon is following in their tracks. In actual fact he was a Sicilian, which I might have suspected from his violent manner, except that I was put off by his red hair. At the moment I first caught sight of him he was engaged in an unfortunate polemic of the type that, as I later learned, he fell into frequently with bureaucrats, officials, and persons of authority. In both arms he was struggling to carry, and with difficulty, since he was a small man, a large black cello-case. The ticket-taker was barring him from the vaporetto on the allegation, a perfectly legal one, that the cello-case due to its bulk was equivalent to a piece of baggage and therefore a ticket must be bought for it exactly as though it were a person. He pointed to a German, an obnoxious person to tell the truth, who had already boarded the vaporetto and was provided with five pieces of baggage and six tickets. Professor Crispi seemed to be contending, rather obscurely, that a cello-case was not the same as a suitcase full of underwear and shirts and some concession was due to art. Another vaporetto was coming up from behind in the canal, the impatient passengers shouted sarcasms in dialect. Finally Professor Crispi, whose gesticulations had for some reason taken the form of a nervous scratching and fumbling inside his overcoat, looked at his hand and found there were two vaporetto tickets in it. It was not clear how this had happened. Possibly there had somehow been another ticket in the lining of his coat that he was not aware of, or perhaps someone, a passenger late to work or the exasperated ticket-taker himself, had slipped the second ticket into his hand. Professor Crispi and the offending object were pushed on board, none too gently under the circumstances, the sailor threw off the line, and the vaporetto chuffed away shoving an impatient white bow-wave ahead of it.

He sat down beside me, cradling the case between his knees, sponged his brow with an unclean handkerchief, and, seeing that I was a foreigner, murmured, "*C'est affreux*," rolling the r in an impressive Sicilian manner. Joining him in French, I agreed that ticket-takers, authorities, and bureaucratic regulations in general were frightful. But the point he clung to was somewhat more precise. A typical monomaniac, he persisted in regarding the incident solely as a rebuff to art in the abstract. "In Germany, sir, or in your country" (what he understood by this term was a total mystery) "a person carrying a musical intrument on the streets is honored, and far from being obliged to purchase a ticket for his instrument, he is often admitted to public conveyances gratis." This seemed so improbable that I was at a loss how to comment on it. Decidedly Professor Crispi was worth cultivating. We went, or more precisely I led him while he clutched the awkward burden he obstinately refused to part with, to Florian's in the Piazza, that curious Jamesian museum of red plush and gilt that seemed to me somehow appropriate to my guest, his dusty complexities, and his general air of anachronism. I took a Campari Soda and he, somewhat to my surprise, a Coca-Cola. "I never take alcohol," he explained, still cradling the cello-case between his knees, "neither do I indulge in coffee or tea. The objection is not on moral grounds. They are simply forbidden to me, as they are to high-wire performers and surgeons who operate on nerves. For those of us engaged in certain professions there are no safety nets." "You are a cellist?" He made a curious gesture, half deprecating and half confidingly menacing, as if he would shortly take his revenge on a world that had condemned him to be something other than what he ought to be. "Ah, I? Nothing so important. A mere human metronome, a sawer of the air with sticks."

His conversation invariably had this same quality, candid and yet with an air of the cryptic about it, giving the impression that he was blurting out his innermost secrets to you as a total stranger and yet lacking in those precise details that would have made it possible to summarize in clear and uncomplicated language what he was trying to say. Gradually his identity, or the cloudy semblance of it, began to take form out of these spasmodic utterances. It was true he was a conductor, as he had implied in his sardonic reference to sawing the air, and he was also a music teacher. But these two trades were only extensions or mutations of his true identity. "I have modeled my life on the Master," he confided to me in a low tone over the table. The Master was Vivaldi, who, as everyone knows, served from 1704 to 1740 as music-master of the Ospedale della Pietà, a Venetian refuge for illegitimate or orphaned girls or those whose parents for whatever reasons were unable to support them. It was an humble station in life for a great composer to occupy, but it did not prevent him from composing a large number (sixty-seven according to Rinaldi's catalog, which is admittedly incomplete) of superb concerti for instruments ranging from the mandoline and piccolo to the *trombo marina*, an enormous seven-foot bowed instrument referred to for some reason, perhaps for irony, as the nun's fiddle.

Professor Crispi's aspirations were not this ambitious, perhaps because he began with greater handicaps. First of all he had been born a Sicilian, and his first task in following in the steps of his model had been to make himself a Venetian. This accomplished, it had been no great feat to procure a position as music teacher in the Municipal Orphanage in Sant'Elena, a suburb or rather a semi-detached island something like a floating kidney appended to the body of the city, and finally to organize an orchestra in this institution. It was a Sisyphean undertaking, because the orphans, the raw material out of which his art was constructed, slipped through his fingers like eels. A female child trained for months to be an oboist would be adopted, or an entire violin section would reach the age of sixteen simultaneously and be sent off to the institution at Verona provided for older girls. The personnel of the orchestra fluctuated madly, and Professor Crispi was obliged to search through the canon of Vivaldi for concerti playable by three flutes and a viola de gamba, or a cembalo without any woodwinds.

On the afternoon I met him, in fact, he had gone to the Conservatory at the other end of the city to borrow a cello in order to rehearse the concerto from *L'Estro armonico* Op. 3 No. 11, which places such demands on the performer that only an instrument of the finest quality can do it justice. The example he held between his legs had been made in Cremona in the eighteenth century, and a good-sized villa in the country could have been bought with its price. I congratulated Professor Crispi on this devotion to his pupils.

"The little girls? Pardon me, Dottore," (all university graduates are called Dottore in Italian) "but you have seized the matter exactly by the wrong end. I do not make music to be kind to little girls any more than Michelangelo made the *David* in order to be kind to his marble." Did he then think of himself as something comparable to Michelangelo? The analogy was not consistent with his earlier summary of himself as a metronome or mere sawer of air, but I did not point this out. In any case I could not, because he had gone on. "If I were to die, or to be removed from office by certain incompetent bureaucrats in the administration of the orphanage who spend their waking hours plotting my downfall, the little girls might be set instead to learning pastry-cooking, or English embroidery, and they would be just as happy. More happy, I would say." (I later came to agree with this judgement perfectly). "No, Dottore, the artist does not engage in art in order to gratify his medium. He engages in it for the sake of art."

I told him I could see his point in regard to sculpture or painting but it seemed to me that in the performing arts the case was somewhat different.

"Different, how?"

"Because in the performing arts, for example in directing a play or conducting an orchestra, one works with human beings instead of inanimate material."

He gave me a long and reflective look before he spoke. "You are perhaps a philanthropist?"

"A literary critic."

"Ah. Well, perhaps these matters are regarded differently in your country. You—*vous autres*" (we were still speaking French) "are devoted, I believe, to the idea of progress." As he spoke this last word his chin protruded a little and his head withdrew between his shoulders, a deprecatory gesture that suggested a resemblance to a chicken. "You are laboring toward a utopia in which nobody is allowed to be poor, sick, wicked, et cetera and everyone will sit happily watching colored shadows on a piece of glass." (Perhaps he had a better idea of my nationality than I thought.) "Your ideal is a state in which everyone is equal to everyone else, that is to say equal to nothing. No pain, suffering, death, all this will be done away with by pharmacology. Excellent. But what then? What will we do then? How will we avoid turning into artichokes or expiring from sheer boredom? You, *vous autres*, Dottore, have lost sight of the fact that the sole reason for obliterating pain, suffering and unhappiness is that the mind and body may be left free to create things of beauty."

He almost had me convinced of this when he reversed himself completely and, with a perverse flicker of a smile, rejected what he had just said as nonsense. "Yet why should we lie to ourselves? In the world as it is presently constructed we are persons of no consequence, you with your poems—" (I don't write poems)—"I with my music. The seats of the mighty are occupied by others. Any vaporetto employee with a gilded band on his hat can command us."

"And you command the little orphans."

He made a dreamy mechanical smile, as though he were really thinking about something else. "It is true I am left with *ce petit coin . . .* this little corner to preside over."

It was not that afternoon that I attended a rehearsal of Professor Crispi's orchestra, but a little later. Presenting myself at his invitation at the orphanage in Sant'Elena, I found no one in charge, the place apparently deserted, and a medley of pseudo-orchestral sounds proceeding from a large hall at one end of the place, which evidently served as a church on Sundays, since there was a rather realistic and grim-looking Crucifix on the wall. The girls were in blue smocks, all with their hair cut exactly the same length. They were on school-benches, and Professor Crispi was on a dais. This last was well, because even elevated above the floor in this way he was scarcely taller than the largest of the girls, a melancholy giantess who was condemned to manipulate a double bass as large as she was. I had feared that the undifferentiated cacophony I had heard from outside the hall was the music itself that the orchestra was attempting to make, but it turned out that they were only tuning.

Professor Crispi gave me his underdone-veal smile, the smile of the Hieronymus Bosch sinner, but spoke not one word to me. Instead he began "sawing the air with a stick," to use his own term. Although at first he *rapped* it, on the stand in front of him, so sharply that all the little girls jumped, and so did I. Then he sawed, and the little girls embarked into the Fourth Concerto for Bassoon and Orchestra in C major, with its opening ritornello as graceful as a ballet of lively swans. Since the perennial shortage in the orchestra at this time was that of a bassoon, I wondered why, under these conditions, he had chosen to rehearse a piece of music which placed emphasis exactly on this instrument—perhaps out of perversity. This lack he made up by giving the part to the cello, which had almost the same range, but a totally different timbre and an incompatible system of fingering. Never mind, the cello would do. The cellist—there was only one, the poor thing—was a girl of about twelve. In order to play the cello properly, a child of her size was obliged first of all to assume an indecent posture with the anthropomorphous instrument lying between her legs, then to flail her right arm back and forth wildly like an epileptic, while at the same time dancing nimbly and with impossible velocity on some sharp strings with her four tender little fingertips. She succeeded in this, or at least kept pace with Professor Crispi's sawing, through the four tutti and three solo sections of the first movement. The largo that followed offered her a little respite. It was graceful as a minuet, with a short iambic motive sounding in the opening measure and iterated from time to time, like a hunting horn echoing from a forest, insofar as a hunting horn can be simulated by a cello.

But the third movement was another allegro, even more ferocious than the first. Again there were four tutti and three solo sections. During the first two of the solo sections she managed to keep the pace, although a veil of perspiration had appeared on her forehead and her limbs were trembling. But in the third solo passage every note was a semiquaver, and there were sixteen of them to a measure. After ten measures or so of this both arms flew into a fit, the left as well as the right, and she gasped and threw her head back and slumped on the bench. The instrument between her legs had conquered her. Professor Crispi, who, as I now recognized, had been humming along with the instrument all along, took over and sang the part to the end of the passage, with an astonishing facility, assuming that he was not a trained vocalist: "Bibibibibibibibi bobobobobobobobo bum-bum-bum-bum BUM bum bum." He seemed not at all angry that the cellist had failed at her terrible task. Yet she shrank as he approached her with baton in hand.

"Oh, Professor."

"Eh?"

Her voice trembled. "You can't play this . . ."

"What?"

"Music . . ."

"What are you saying?"

"On a . . ."

"Stop! Don't speak!"

"On a cello!" she finished desperately, and then collapsed into sobs.

He came around behind her bench. The cellist, and all the other girls, continued to stare straight ahead. The Crucified Savior on the wall gazed down on the whole scene. From directly behind the unfortunate cellist Professor Crispi raised the baton, in the gesture of a Roman gladiator. The baton came down. It struck the bench just at the side of the cellist, and shattered into two pieces. Corporal punishment was forbidden by the Criminal Code. Professor Crispi was after all not a criminal. Yet even I flinched at the terrible sound of the baton breaking; I could almost rather have been struck than to hear that sharp and pitiless pistol-crack in my ears. Did Professor Crispi, in this administering justice to the malefactor, regret the loss of his baton? Not at all. He left the broken pieces on the floor where they were, and went to a kind of umbrella stand by the dais where he had a dozen or more fresh ones at hand. There were several other pieces of broken batons, as I now saw, strewn around the floor of the hall. Professor Crispi raised the new baton. "The Concerto in B flat major," he said. "The one," he said, "with the allegro passage for double bass." The giantess blanched.

Professor Crispi offered to accompany me back to my lodgings in San Cassiano, not far from the Rialto. I never did succeed in finding out where he himself lived. Perhaps near me, which would have accounted for his accompanying me, or perhaps in the municipal madhouse, which was at the other end of Venice, exactly symmetrical to the orphanage. We did not arrive, however, at either of these destinations. Along the way he kept up a constant stream of talk, up and down the bridges, along the narrow calli, around the many corners. Yet he seemed to be meditating with himself rather than speaking directly to me. "To weave gold out of straw . . ." I caught. "To carve Davids out of sand, to make silk purses out of sows' daughters with ten thumbs for fingers . . ." Then he did address me directly, seeming to perceive me for the first time. "You were aware," he inquired cautiously, "of deficiencies in the third movement of the C major concerto?" "Not at all," I told him. "It was lovely, particularly the largo." "That is the second movement. In the third movement . . ."

He stopped, and seemed to be no longer aware that I was present. We had arrived at a quarter of the city near the church of Saints Giovanni and Paolo, which the Venetians, in their soft laziness and their love of buzzing sounds, call San Zanipolo. From somewhere, a window of a nearby house perhaps, we heard something that sounded like an old-fashioned French taxi horn, except that it had gone mad and gyrated gracefully up and down the musical scale. He stood as immovable as a statue and listened. Very slowly he slipped his hands into his overcoat pockets. With a solemn expression he gradually raised his chin, until his head was held erect in the posture of a triumphant general, or a Saint perceiving a vision. There was a little bridge like a crescent moon in front of us, and across the rio was a palazzo. It was from the window of this palazzo that the sound was proceeding. It resembled, not only a mad taxicab, but also somehow a cello fitted with a reed and played with the breath, and at the same time a hunting horn echoing in the forest. There was an acerbic, twangy, and archaic timbre to it; it was a sound like a baritone oboe, or the baying of a laryngitic hound. It was oddly beautiful. I too stood transfixed by the oddness, by the beauty, by the slightly arcane magic of the moment.

At last Professor Crispi spoke, while continuing to listen with the same intensity.

"The little fingers," he said, "are having difficulty reaching the B flat."

I couldn't imagine how he could tell merely from the sound that the performer was a child. But presently the music stopped, and a moment later his oracular prophecy was exactly fulfilled. At the large ovigal window of the palazzo appeared a little girl perhaps nine. She was a sad-faced thing with large eyes, as pretty and as touching as a figurine in china. With a sibylline calm, remarkable for one so young, she noticed us standing by the bridge and caught Professor Crispi's eye.

Before I could stop him he bolted across the bridge and disappeared into the door of the palazzo. I remained where I was. From the depths of the stone palace I heard the sound of an old-fashioned bell operated by a cord-pull. Then nothing, for five minutes or so. I lingered, my eyes falling finally to the water of the rio. All the water in the canals of Venice is stagnant but this was a particularly putrid one. It was an interesting color—greenish, slightly greasy, in the iridescent and polychrome manner of Paul Sérusier and the Pont-Aven group. There was a former cat in it, and some devices used to prevent the conception of children. I thought how odd it was that the sordid in our world was so mingled with the luxurious, and with the most exquisite forms of art. It was a very fine palazzo indeed; surely those who lived in it were wealthy and important people. From the ovigal window

I could detect the sounds of a fracas. Voices were raised; one of them was Professor Crispi's, unmistakable in its reediness and oboe-like timbre. The one word I could catch was the word "No," which is the same in all languages, except for German where it varies only slightly to *nein*. Then Professor Crispi was projected from the doorway. His hat was on crooked and his overcoat askew. His face was no longer underdone veal but raw beefsteak. "*C'est affreux*," I heard him mumble under his breath. I stayed behind the bridge and he didn't see me. He assumed, evidently, that I had gone on home by myself, which was certainly what I ought to have done much earlier.

In spite of this setback—this *affreux contretemps*—Professor Crispi managed in some way to arrange another interview with the Baladrins, as the owners of the impressive palazzo were called, and this time he persuaded me to accompany him. "You, a poet, can speak with eloquence." he argued.

I had given up trying to explain to him that I was not a poet. "Not in Italian," I protested. But it was no use. Meeting me at Florians'—in order not to reveal where he lived, perhaps, and not to admit that I lived anywhere—he towed me after him to the San Zanipolo quarter, grumbling to himself all the way about the difficulty of making bricks without straw, and gold with straw—it was all a bit disconnected. The Baladrins, mother and father, received us correctly but distantly. Commendatore Baladrin was a prominent solicitor, with a distinguished name that went back to the Battle of Lepanto. He was a stiff and stuffy bursting sort of man, with a waxed mustache which he was able to twitch at will. His wife was a queenly figure with a monobosom in the Victorian style, much given to smiling sweetly. Emilia, their daughter, was visible in the shadows at the bottom of the room, only her large liquid eyes showing any signs of life; the rest of her was an inanimate puppet. Against the wall stood her instrument, which always has the facility of surprising us, no matter how many times we have seen one before. More than a musical instrument it suggested a hookah for smoking opium, perhaps, or some antique weapon of warcraft. Out of the top of it came the thin curved tube of the mouthpiece, and there was an incomprehensible system of levers and valves along its barrel. I didn't know why it was not put away in its case. Perhaps Emilia had been practicing on it as we arrived; she had a look about her as though she were, not so much out of breath, but spiritually exhausted. She said not a word during our conversation with her parents. We were shown in by a maid in a starched uniform, who then left.

Lacking a baton, Professor Crispi sawed the air with his hand. Perhaps later he would use it to strike—not Commendatore Baladrin, since corporal punishment was forbidden—but the back of the chair in which Commendatore Baladrin was sitting. "I have brought my friend"—he pointed to me—"the well-known English poet." He still didn't know my name; he never paid attention to what other people were saying. I didn't bother to explain that I was not English and not a poet. I have no idea who the Baladrins thought I was. Perhaps Professor Crispi's roommate at the municipal madhouse. Signora Baladrin smiled at me, gently, in the way that one smiles at someone who has an affliction, or does not speak the language of the country.

Commendatore Baladrin was quite firm in his stand on the matter. After all he was a lawyer and an eminent one, and especially trained in adversary argument. "The key to our objection," he said, "which I am trying to make clear to you, Professor Crispi, is that Emilia is not an orphan. We do not therefore see why she should frequent an orphanage."

His wife joined in, "We explained that to you at our previous . . ."

Yes, yes. That was a painful memory. "I have another proposition," muttered Professor Crispi almost inaudibly. "She could become a day pupil."

"There is no precedent for day pupils in an orphanage," Commendatore Baladrin stated flatly. "Either a child is an orphan or she is not."

"And besides," said Signora Baladrin sweetly, "Emilietta does not really enjoy her lessons. We have almost decided on our own to terminate them."

Lessons?

Yes. We were told that Commendatore Baladrin himself, who had been trained in the instrument in his youth, was instructing Emilia as a diversion for both of them in their leisure hours. In fact, the very instrument leaning against the wall—the Signora pointed—was the one he had played in his younger days.

"It is in bad condition, I can see a crack in it from here, and lessons by amateurs are worthless."

"Carla," said Signora Baladrin just as sweetly, "show Professor Crispi the door."

The maid appeared and showed Professor Crispi the door. I came along too, naturally. "Ah, so this is the door," said Professor Crispi, gazing at it with interest. "Very beautiful."

I couldn't tell whether this was sarcasm or not. Either one case or the other was true: that he was incapable of sarcasm, or that everything he said was sarcasm. Or perhaps both at once.

"It is even more impressive from the outside," Signora Baladrin suggested in her dulcet tones.

Very prudently, I hadn't said a word during the visit, even though I was a well-known English poet, possessing eloquence.

That ended the matter, as I thought. It certainly should have, but it didn't. It was perhaps a week later that, making my way home across the Rialto bridge, I saw an elegant red-and-white speedboat coming toward me up the Grand Canal at high speed. One of the charms of Venice, of course, is that things that are done in all the other cities of the world by wheeled vehicles are done here by boats. Refrigerators, grand pianos, and stage sets for the opera at the Fenice are delivered in boats, and the hearses that carry the dead to the cemetery at San Michele are boats. Even the taxis are sleek mahogany motoboats, polished like yachts. This particular boat, moving at a velocity not permitted to other watercraft, and setting the water of the Canal to slapping the old stone palazzi at its edge, was a medical speedboat from the Civil Hospital, not so much an ambulance as a Venetian equivalent of a paramedic van. It turned into a small rio not far from the bridge, sending a shower of spray onto the stones. It was followed only a moment or two later by a blue speedboat belonging to the Carabinieri, which executed the same interesting maneuver. Everybody turned and looked, and people began walking, as they will in Venice or anywhere else in the world, in the direction of the apparent incident. I went with them. Unlike the others, who were merely curious in a spectator sort of way, I had a premonition. I followed the two speedboats, I like to tell myself, chiefly in the hope of reassuring myself that my premonition was mistaken. In this I was not successful.

Sure enough, the two boats had stopped in the rio by the Palazzo Baladrin, exactly by the graceful little bridge in the shape of a crescent moon. Even though the boats had preceded me only by a minute or two, a considerable crowd had collected by this time. One of those standing before the doorway proved to be the maid Carla, who had apparently come out into the crowd to demonstrate her talents as a kind of rhapsode or bard, to narrate or mime the events that only a short time before had taken place inside. "*L'ha fatto freddamente*," she repeated several times. "He did it coldly. Not in passion. He did it coldly." Evidently, in her sense of drama, everything ought to be done with passion, and it was this detail of the event that shocked her most deeply. For myself I was not surprised. I remembered Professor Crispi, quite *freddamente* and without passion, breaking his baton over the back of the child cellist's bench.

He himself was the first to appear in the doorway—without passion and showing only his unusual expression of contempt for persons of authority, in this case the two Carabinieri who were carrying him, practically, by the elbows. His hands were shackled in front of him, and a piece of chain ran around behind his body and appeared again on the other side. He didn't catch my eye as they put himn in the blue speedboat. I was glad of this. I caught a glimpse of him pronouncing to himself one of those French words that you make by pursing your lips as though you were playing a flute—perhaps *affreux*. The he disappeared into the boat There was a wait, and a fourth actor in the drama appeared. An officer of Carabinieri came out of the palazzo with a small and elegant revolver, a woman's weapon really, which he held carefully by the barrel in a handkerchief. This I though was an extraordinary piece of police practice. I had hung about the scenes of a number of crimes, in America and elsewhere, in the hope of seeing something interesting come out the door, but nowhere in the world had I seen a policeman carrying out the fatal weapon in full view of the interested spectators. Perhaps all the world is a drama to the Mediterranean peoples, which might account for some of their attractions as well as for certain ghastly incidents in their history. The revolver-bearing officer got into the blue boat with the others, and it burbled away down the rio and disappeared.

We were still waiting. There was something else to come. What was it? Ah! here it was. Carla explained the cast of characters to the spectators. Emilietta appeared, red-eyed, with a shawl over her head, accompanied by a female relative. She looked straight ahead of her and paid no attention to the murmurs that accompanied her as the two of them made their way through the crowd toward the waiting mahogany water-taxi.

"*Poveretta!*"

"Poor little orphan!"

"*Peccato!*"

Which means both, it's a sin, and isn't it too bad, a particularly useful word. The water-taxi, with its more elegant exhaust-note, disappeared down the rio as the blue Carabinieri boat had. It was over. There was nothing more to wait for, yet the crowd dispersed only slowly, as such crowds will. People stayed to comment, shrewdly and extensively, on the drama and on the characters, motives, and probably fate of the participants. As for Commendatore Baladrin and his wife, their fate was fixed. They were going to San Michele in a black boat.

I never saw Professor Crispi again, and I am unacquainted with all the details of his subsequent fate, but needless to say his extravagant gesture was unavailing. Orphans can not be manufactured, or if they are, the manufacturer can hope to derive but little good from it. That is the way of the world, just as one must but a ticket if he wishes to carry a cello onto a vaporetto. We may wish the world were different, but certain laws operate. As for the little girls in the orphanage, no doubt they were set to doing something different, such as pastry-cooking or English embroidery. Perhaps they were happier for it; I like to think so. Several weeks later I did learn something about Emilietta, partly from an item in the newspaper and partly from a café waiter, as a matter of fact—by this time everyone in Venice was discussing the details. It seemed, from piecing together these various sources of information, that a court had remanded her to the custory of relatives in Verona who held the firm belief that music was interdicted for little children, since it was good for the soul but bad for the character. This is a doctrine which, I believe, is found in Saint Augustine or somewhere else. The café waiter told me that the Verona relatives—two unmarried sisters—were very pious. And no doubt Emilietta, in her time, became the same.

THE MARTYRED POET

This happened toward the end of my stay in Xanadu. By that time I had become quite the chum of Chairman Khan, so much that I was indispensable to him in the management of state affairs. This came about because I was the only person who could curb his uncontrollable rages. I did this simply by agreeing with him. I too would get angry, in fact angrier than the Chairman himself. Our anger mounted and mounted. We shook our fists, stamped on the floor, and broke pottery. "That bastard!" he would shout. And I: "Yes, and furthermore he . . ." and so on. I always topped him in his rage. When he was finally bested, the Chairman would invariably say, "Well, I wouldn't go that far." Then he would calm down and attempt to quell my excessive passion.

I never revealed this secret to anyone, and since the rages always took place in private the secret never came out. All the others who attempted to deal with Chairman Khan under these circumstances, from personal valets to ministers of state, simple disappeared from sight and were never seen again. He said of me, "Polo's a good fellow. He has some sense in his head. You can count on what he says being right. Of course, he has a bad temper, and sometimes allows it to get out of control."

About a month before I left Cathay I was having tea with the Chairman on the terrace of the Pleasure Dome, his official residence in the capital. He had a private brass band to play at teatime and there were colored umbrellas to keep off the sun; it was really quite pleasant. Somehow or other the conversation got onto literature and I began telling him about Kafka. His story about an animal who lives in a burrow. The one about a fellow who tried to get into a castle but couldn't. Another one about a fellow who is executed even though his crime is never explained to him. He found all this highly entertaining.

Then, out of sheer mischief, I began telling him about the punishment machine in the tale *The Penal Colony*, which is adjusted by an officer so that it engraves the criminal's sentence all over his body, and suggesting that he might have such a machine constructed in Cathay. He took a lively interest in this. We agreed that it wouldn't really be possible to inscribe the culprit's crime on his flesh, because some crimes, while not serious, are very complex (embezzling small amounts of money from the tax accounts), and others while heinous are quite simple. But perhaps an inscription that was merely decorative or symbolic could be used, like the Blessed Seal of the Commonweal, which was in the form of a giant scarab.

"That sounds all very good and well. Could we have this fellow Kafka come and serve as advisor to our judiciary?"

"No, unfortunately he died of tuberculosis."

"Ah well, we don't have that any more since the Glorious Rotation. We stick pins in people."

"Besides, he did seem to disapprove of the machine he was describing."

"So do I," said the Chairman. "I disapprove of all forms of punishment, no matter what apparatus they require. But it is necessary, so one might as well have the best equipment obtainable."

The Execution Machine in Xanadu was in a public square, which was called Poppyseed Square, after a slogan of the Glorious Rotation: "The Empire is a single sword; the people are a million poppyseeds." Out of curiosity I went a few days later to see it in operation. During the times when it was not in use, it was left in place, since it was sturdy and permanently mounted and there was nothing on it for anyone to steal. The bronze in time had acquired a beautiful patina and the whole thing resembled some immense and odd abstract sculpture. When the time for its use arrived, it was necessary only for the executioner to sharpen the ends of the twenty bronze chisels with a file.

A number of crimes in Cathay were punishable by death, ranging from violence against an official to the construction of telescopes and microscopes. When a person was guilty of any of these acts, he was immediately put into a death cell without any trial at all. There he waited until twenty condemned men had accumulated; no more, no less. Women were not subject to capital punishment; instead females guilty of any infraction of the laws were taken to the Pleasure Dome and there violated by Chairman Khan; although, since he was in his sixties by the time I knew him, in most cases he delegated this symbolic act to one of the several hundred Officers of the Guard who had qualified themselves for the task. Although I myself was present once when Chairman Khan personally violated an actress, one whose name was famous throughout the land, for the misdemeanor of striking her servant with a *ch'an-fui* or mulberry-tree switch—a custom which dated from before the Rotation and was considered reactionary and demeaning to servants. I believe however that the Chairman in this instance was motivated not by concupiscence—since I knew him to be a person of the highest probity—but by a sense of duty and a determination to make an example of the actress in question; to show that even famous personalities were not immune to the punishments provided by law. To delegate this task to a Guards officer might have given pleasure to the officer; this was the real reason for Chairman Khan's intervention in this case.

But back to capital punishment, and the Execution Machine. Its most important parts were a cylinder of bronze and a heavy piston, about the dimensions of an ordinary bucket. The piston was connected through a complicated system of levers and pivots to twenty sharp bronze blades, which in turn slipped into twenty bronze rings fixed around the necks of the condemned men, who stood in a row a meter or more apart. The cylinder was loaded with a charge of gunpowder, an officer applied a lighted punk to the touch-hole, and there was a loud bang from the cylinder. The twenty bronze blades were driven instantaneously and with terrific force into the vertebral columns of the twenty condemned men, just below the base of the head.

The twenty men were not bound or confined in any way except that their necks were held immovable in the bronze rings. Thus while waiting for the final moment they were free to do whatever they wanted. Some made speeches to the spectators defending their acts, some pled for mercy, and one calmly read a newspaper provided him by an officer, although I suspect this was an act of pure bravado. One grimaced, spat, and yelled that Chairman Khan was a mother-fucker, and another masturbated furiously with his two free hands. Nobody paid any attention to him. The officer touched his punk to the end of the cylinder, the gunpowder banged, and the twenty men jerked in unison like electrified frogs. The twenty heads slumped and the limbs went limp.

Yet I had the suspicion, as I watched, that perhaps severing the vertebral column at the cervical level does not immediately terminate consciousness; and this theory was confirmed by Professor Hai-Ni, the physician whose job it was to oversee the medical aspects of the ceremony. "The cerebral circulation is uninterrupted," he told me, "since the blade is designed to slip between the jugulars without severing them. Death results fron anoxia and consequent cessation of cerebral activity. I would estimate the average persistence of consciousness at seven minutes."

"During which the condemned man thinks of what?"

"I have no idea."

I was curious and hung around to see what was done with the bodies. I found they were used for research by the University medical department, and what was left was pulverized and used for fertilizer at the Experimental Nenuphar Station, in the marshes just on the outskirts of the city. The curators of the station, in their turn, were conducting experiments to see whether the heinousness of the crime committed by the felons affected the colors of the nenuphars; whether murderers produced black flowers, for instance, or adulterous lovers pink or violet ones. This station grew the most exquisite water lilies in the country, although it was not yet established whether this had anything to do with the fertilizer.

This, and Professor Hai-Ni's remarks about consciousness, led me to an experiment of my own. The next time I had tea with Chairman Khan, I steered the conversation onto capital punishment, and he explained to me the rationale for the Machine in Poppyseed Square. Gunpowder, it goes without saying, was invented in Cathay, and the Machine had been in use for over seven hundred years. The reason he kept it around, even though it might seem somewhat anachronistic, was to remind people constantly that gunpowder kills. In Poppyseed Square they could see it killing—killing their own countrymen, people they knew, their own neighbors, men they had passed in the street. If gunpowder were used for cannon, then it would kill foreigners, and kill them at a distance. As cannon were more and more improved, they would kill them at greater and greater distances, until at last no one noticed that the cannons were killing people, and they would only admire their complexity, their accuracy, and the distance at which they could operate. Consequently, Chairman Khan had not accepted the advice of his Military Council to convert the Execution Machine into a weapon of war, he told me with considerable satisfaction, putting some cream into his Lapsong Souchong.

I told him I agreed thoroughly with his policy. And then I shrewdly introduced my proposed experiment into the conversation, at just the right point. As soon as I mentioned the name of Lu Po he flew into a temper. I flew into an even greater temper, and so on. I have already explained how this was done. "Calm down, Polo," he told me. "This poet is a despicable vermin. But you go too far."

He gave me carte blanche to work with Professor Hai-Ni in setting up the experiment. The Professor was a neurosurgeon at the University of the Glorious Rotation, a bald man in his fifties with a peculiarly shaped head, with a ridge along it like a roof, and a perpetually disagreeable expression. To be candid, he looked like an iguana with a toothache. However, he was an excellent neurosurgeon.

As soon as he grasped the point of my experiment, we went together to explain it to the subject. He was the nineteenth man in the death cell; they were waiting for the twentieth. Lu Po had been a celebrated poet in Cathay from the time of the Glorious Rotation. It was he who in former years had composed the ceremonial ode, "In Xanadu did Chairman Khan a stately Pleasure Dome decree." More lately, however, he had turned satirical, and he was to be executed on account of a poem about the Chairman in which he referred to the copious dog droppings around the capital as "Khan Do."

"You have an interesting name," I told him. "In my language it means wolf."

"Well, in my language it means a reflection from heavenly waters."

"It's lucky you're a Cathayan then and not a Venetian. It may be that names have an influence on character."

"Well, if they're going to execute me in any case, what's the difference? Might as well be killed for a wolf as for a reflection from heavenly waters."

Professor Hai-Ni intervened in this semantic discussion and explained the experiment to him. He said, "It would mean living a little bit longer."

"You call that a life?"

"Well, it's a kind of life."

We did not want to do anything without the consent of the subject. In any case, his cooperation was essential. He finally agreed.

As soon as the cylinder banged and the bodies jerked, a half-dozen physicians and assistants rushed forward and quickly removed the body of Lu Po. They laid it on the ground and deftly made two incisions, then they inserted tubes and started a blood supply moving into the jugulars. The assistants held up jars of blood, then the whole business was put into a sedan chair, and the bunch of them went off at a quick trot to the University hospital. Professor Hai-Ni and I followed.

In the hospital the head was skillfully severed and mounted on a stand. The assistants continued to pump blood into it with the aid of a device worked by small ivory levers. Stimulus from acupuncture needles was then applied, and Lu Po came to in only a few minutes.

His first words were, "My neck hurts."

Everyone had been waiting breathlessly for some message from the beyond. Professor Hai-Ni said, "Please tell us something that is not so self-evident."

His second remark was, "I have an erection."

"That's only imaginary."

"Well, please provide me with an imaginary playmate."

"Don't talk dirt."

"Well, I do feel rotten. How long does this have to go on?"

Professor Hai-Ni explained again the whole point of the experiment, which was to test his imagination and creative powers under these unusual conditions. "We'd like you," he said, "to compose a poem for us. And, to expiate your terrible crime, we'd like you to write a poem this time in praise of, rather than mocking, our Glorious Chairman."

"In praise of?"

"In praise of."

"He doesn't have many lovable qualities."

"Think of something."

"It's not my style. I'm a satirist now."

"Well then, we'll just wait. We can do experiments on how often your eyelids flutter."

"I have pains in several limbs, none of which exist. If you'll allow me to pass into oblivion, I'll do anything you say."

The poem took him several hours, because the subject was a difficult one. As he himself said, the Chairman was not a promising subject for encomium. Finally he produced a poem in the form of the classic Imperial ode, in tetrameter octets with an unrhyming opening line (called the Tribute) and the rest of it rhyming xbabaaab. When it was finished it was not too preposterously silly, and contained no easily discernable underlying ironies. And here is how it went, with some details of the composition process.

"All hail our blessed Chairman Khan,
The leader of our Nation;
The man whose slightest chance remark
Provokes our wild elation."

"I'm not sure this is going to do," said Professor Hai-Ni.

"The one who found us in the dark,
Who pressed our noses to . . ."

"Careful."

"Who pressed our noses to the mark;
Whose works the very dogs that bark . . ."

"I'd stay away from dogs if I were you."

"If I'm going to stay away from dogs, then 'bark' is out. The only other rhyme is 'lark.'"

"Very well, try 'lark.'"

"And for the ending, I have admiration, ovation, and ejaculation."

"Once again, I would beware of the last."

The poet tried further:

"Whose soul is thripple as the lark . . ."

"Get a grip on your yourself, man. There's no such word as thripple."

"Whose mind is supple as a lark?"

"That's a word all right, but I'm not sure larks are supple."

"Are you a literary critic or a neurosurgeon?"

"Very well, go on."

"All right, you don't like supple." Lu Po, or his head, closed its eyes and frowned.

"Whose mind

(I'm also considering soul)

is agile as a lark."

"I don't care for that," said the Professor. "It suggests that our Chairman is tricky or that his thought processes are hard to follow."

"Whose mind as lofty as the lark . . ."

"Well, that's not too bad. It all depends on the last line. Which rhymes in *ation*."

"Commands our admiration. Hah!"

"It doesn't command our admiration. That implies that there is something compulsory in our admiration of him."

"H'mm. I see your point." He thought again. "Bestirs our admiration?"

"Now that's plain silly."

"I have it! Deserves our admiration."

This too suggested thought-control, or the notion that the admiration felt by the Nation for Chairman Khan was less than totally spontaneous. After a conference in whispers between the medical and political experts, it was concluded that Lu Po's cerebral matter was deteriorating and his poetry was only going to get worse instead of better. It was therefore decided to settle for "lark" and "deserves."

Professor Hai-Ni said, "I suppose that will do. I'm shutting down the machine, Lu Po."

"Farewell all," said the poet.

THE PHOTOGRAPH

Boris was handsome. He might easily have made friends or found a girl for himself. Others did, without any particular attributes or qualities different from his. But each person is different, not so much in what he looks like on the outside, or whether he is handsome or ugly, but in what he wants on the inside. What Boris liked was to receive letters from a friend. Such letters weren't the same at all as the ordinary circulars, advertisements, and bills that came every day in the mail, most of which you could dispose of by dropping them in the wastebasket. When you got a letter that your friend had written for you alone, and sealed so that nobody else could read it, there was an excitement about holding the white envelope in your hands, only a little soiled from its passage through the postal service, and delaying, even, for a few seconds the moment when you would tear it open, or better yet cut it with a knife, to read the intimate thoughts your friend had chosen to transmit to you in this public and perilous and yet secret way, passing through many hands and hazards and surrendering itself in the end only to the one person to whom it was consecrated by the legend written on the outside. Opening such a letter was a consummation, a highest mystery of body and soul.

The trouble was that Boris had no friends in other cities who might send him such letters. If they were in other cities, how would he meet them? And if they were in his own city —where he might make friends easily, considering his attractions, his agreeable manners, and the comfortable allowance that provided him with adequate pocket money—what reason would they have to write him letters? Instead what arrived every day was the epitome of banality: trash of various kinds, circulars, bank statements, and ads for erotic materials. In addition there was a letter now and then from his old professor inquiring as to what he was doing. "Dear Boris, and so forth, I've been wondering what you are doing these days and how you are fulfilling your promise. Your brilliant work on the tropes of Guillaume de Loris," and so on. He dropped this in the wastebasket along with the usual letter from his aunt. The aunt was fat and short of breath and had never married. She had little to do with herself except write him letters of a monitory and moralistic tendency, tempered by a certain playfulness which she deemed appropriate for a youthful correspondent. In addition to calling his attention to good books which she thought might interest him, like *The Imitation of Christ* and *Silas Marner*, she always ended by cautioning him to regularity in a certain intimate habit, a line of advice that bored him profoundly.

The bank statement he balanced, the circulars went into the wastebasket along with the aunt and the professor. How was he to find his way out of this impasse, this quagmire and vicious circle? Against all probability it was the aunt who helped him, not overtly or in any way beknownst to herself, but in the image he held of her in his thoughts. "To get a letter write a letter." He could hear her saying this, with her trite and yet irrefutable common sense. Boris rummaged around in his desk and found some writing-paper, in good condition except that the piece on the bottom was a little soiled. The top piece was immaculate. Once he was settled down with this sheet on the desk in front of him—what a delight, its blankness and smoothness, its passive and even self-humiliating acceptance of whatever he chose to write on it—the task went quite easily. He was finished in a quarter of an hour and signed his name with a flourish. The envelope was of the same white paper as the letter itself. He knew it would be soiled somewhat in its passage across the city through the postal service, but even this thought gave him pleasure, especially since he knew that the letter inside would be protected by this very soiling of the envelope and arrive at its destination in the same pristine and virginal state in which it left his hands. Last, the stamp. In moistening this with a sponge (he disliked touching foreign objects to his lips) and applying it to the envelope he was conscious of the fact that it signified the readiness of a powerful agency of the government to carry the letter through rain, snow, darkness, and other environmental perils, and that henceforth it would be against the law for anyone to open it except the person to whom it was addressed, and this too gave him satisfaction. Then he put on his coat and went out to the corner to mail it. When he raised it to the slot the box seemed to suck it abruptly and rather impatiently out of his hands, as though there were a vacuum inside. This displeased him a little. He would have preferred to hold it in his fingers for a while longer, letting it slip from them only gradually in the way that lovers (at least in the movies) separate in train stations, their bodies, then their arms, and last their fingers slipping apart in the tremulous and melancholy delight of parting. But the box seemed anxious to get the letter started on its way and seized it almost rudely from his hands.

The next day there was nothing. But there were often delays in the postal service, and he had told himself that he might have to be patient and wait for several days for the letter he was expecting. On the second day it came: a white envelope sealed and addressed to him personally in handwriting. Turning it over in his hands, he felt a warm rising tide of expectation that was almost painful. He started to tear it open with his fingers, but he restrained himself. Instead he found a nailfile (he didn't for some reason possess a letter-knife), inserted it carefully under the flap at one end, and sawed away with a reciprocal motion until the envelope was open. Although the letter was short he went on poring over it for some time, fixing each word in his mind and examining the handwriting in the possibility that it concealed some significance he had not noticed at first.

Then, when he began to exhaust this pleasure, it occurred to him that he had forgotten another pleasure that still lay ahead of him: that of answering. But not too quickly, something cautioned him. To reply to his friend's letter the same day might betray an eagerness on his part, or give the impression he had nothing to do except write letters to him, and this might lead his friend to conclude that he was an unimportant person who was really not worth cultivating in a serious way. It was necessary, on the contrary, to give the impression that he had many other things to do and could only get around to answering letters of this kind the second or third day, although he might apologize in the opening lines for the delay. He wrote a first draft that afternoon, therefore, and revised it and made a clean copy for mailing the next morning. "My dear friend, what a pleasure to get your letter. I'm sorry I haven't answered it sooner, but I've had many things to do. Financial affairs regarding my bank, a letter from my aunt and another from a former professor who is still interested in my career, and so on. My dear friend, how are you? Tell me something about yourself. I know so little about you. Can you recommend any good books? Recently I've been reading *Silas Marner*, and I also plan to read *The Imitation of Christ* when I have time. Do you go out with girls very much? Or do you prefer friends? I hope it's the latter. (I shouldn't say this when I've know you for so short a time, but I'll dare to anyhow.) What do you look like? Are you hand-handsome? Please send a photograph. (It doesn't matter if you're not handsome; there are other things that are more important, such as good books or discussing about ideas.) Hoping to hear from you soon, your friend Boris." This letter he slipped into the box confidently, not bothering to let it linger in his hands before it fell into the slot.

When the mail came Boris pored over the letter for a long time, as he had with the first one. He was sure his friend was handsome, but he was not quite sure either. And also that he preferred friends to girls, although the letter hadn't been very specific about this. On the whole he was pleased with the course events were taking, and whenever he passed a mirror he noticed he was going around with a little smile on his face all the time, especially on one side.

That afternoon he put on his coat and tie and went out to the Grand City Bazaar. The photo machine, he remembered, was on the third floor. It was a kind of little detached closet or cubicle of gray metal, with a curtain for privacy and an adjustable seat like a piano stool. He was not quite sure how it worked. But the instructions, which were designed to be understood even by persons of limited intelligence, were quite clear. He adjusted the piano stool to the proper height and sat down on it, read over the instructions once more, and put the coin in the machine. For a moment nothing happened. Then there was a brilliant white flash, as violent as a bolt of lightning. This made him blink a little, but it was over quickly and it hadn't been as bad as he thought. Then there was another flash, and a third, and a fourth. This he hadn't expected. He was like a boxer who confidently receives a blow to the jaw, congratulating himself that it was no worse and that he is still in fairly good shape, and then finds himself overwhelmed by the rain of blows that follows it, directed by a shrewd opponent who sees a momentary weakness and knows how to take advantage of it. He tried to keep from flinching, since the apparatus might still be taking his picture. But after the fourth flash the machine was quiet.

His vision affected by various black spots and quiverings, he waited for what was to come next. There was a clicking in the entrails of the machine, and a gurgle of running fluids. After a short while the apparatus ejected a slightly damp strip of paper with four photographs on it. At first Boris didn't recognize himself. If there had been only one photograph he might have been pleased with it or at least accepted it, seeing there were no alternatives, but when there were four he didn't care much for any of them. The first one was nervous, the next two were cringing from the blows of white lightning, and so on. After reflection he decided that the fourth one might do. It showed a face stricken by adversity but responding with fortitude and even a proud stoicism, the lower lip caught slightly in the teeth in a way that suggested determination. As soon as the strip of paper was dry he put it in his pocket. Back home in his apartment he cut off the fourth photograph and sent it to his friend.

For several days nothing happened. He even began to forget

his friend, a little, and got out his old notes on Guillaume de Loris to see if he might perhaps write a scholarly article on them. Then, when he had almost stopped expecting it, a letter came. The weekend had intervened, he now realized, and there were no mail deliveries on Saturday and Sunday. His old excitement mounting inside him again, he tore open the envelope and took out the photograph.

He couldn't decide whether his friend was handsome or not. He saw a lean, pointed, foxlike face, the lower lip caught slightly in the teeth on one side and the glance rather uncertain. The fox after all was an intelligent and beautiful animal. It was true that people hunted it, but they were despicable boors who were looked down upon by people of cultivated taste. There were many ways of being handsome, and his friend was handsome in his way. He was glad he was not handsome in some banal and insipid way, but exactly in the way that he was.

He put the photograph in the frame of the bathroom mirror, where he could look at it as he shaved every morning, and after a while an odd thing began happening. At first the face in the photograph had been that of a stranger. But gradually his own face in the mirror, which was so familiar to him before that he had hardly bothered to look at it as he shaved, began to resemble the face in the photograph more and more. All photographs are the photographs of strangers, he reflected. Some poet, perhaps Rimbaud or Guillaume de Loris, had said *Je est un autre.* In his own mind his friend was ordinary, but photographed and put into the frame of the mirror he became ordinary in another way, an unusual way. His friend, by having himself photographed, had *become a stranger and so existed.* Because we don't exist for ourselves; only the others around us exist and our own self is like the water in our mouth, without taste and invisible. His friend didn't exist for himself and he, Boris, didn't exist for himself. That was why it was terrible living without a friend, because you were tasteless and invisible, like the water in your own mouth. But when you had a friend and sent him your photo, or he sent you his, then you became strangers and yet strangers who knew each other intimately, that is, *beings who exist*. Boris smiled as he regarded the photograph in the mirror, his smile became an excitement and finally he cut himself with the razor. A drop of blood collected and trickled slowly down his face; he was like the letter he had ripped open with the nailfile, he had opened his body to his friend and he was no longer alone. The photograph watched him intently while this happened, its glance fixed first on his eyes and then on the blood. Still smiling, he applied a piece of cotton to the wound and went into the other room to dress with the cotton still sticking to his cheek.

That afternoon he went back to the Grand City Bazaar, this time to a stand in the cosmetics department called "For Monsieur." There he bought a bottle of cologne, a small one but the most expensive brand, which was called Narcisse. The clerk was the kind of a girl he thought he might like to have, if he ever had a girl. She was slender and dark, with very dark eyes which she had intensified even more with lines drawn with a special kind of pencil. The only trouble was that she had colored her eyelids blue, which Boris disliked. He wanted to tell her, "If I'm going to have you you mustn't color your eyelids blue, it's out of the question and you look much better simply like yourself." But of course it was his having her that was out of the question; they had hardly even spoken to each other and she probably had other concerns in her life, as Boris did himself. Still she was quite pretty and not ordinary at all. It was hard to say what would have happened if he had told her this about her eyes. She might have been angry, or worse simply laughed at him, but she might have taken the blue color off her eyelids and it would have been the start of a whole new way of life for Boris.

He didn't say this, however, partly because he was embarrassed by the thought that she might think he was buying the cologne for himself, and also because he was distracted by the small and yet somehow alive and mouselike shapes that he now noticed stirring in her blouse. When he gave her the money she smiled at him in her particular way, and to make it clear the package wasn't for himself he told her he would like it gift-wrapped.

"Very good."

"And also wrapped for mailing."

"We can mail it directly from the store."

He agreed to this idea, which would save him a lot of trouble, and gave her the address. He thanked her for all this perhaps too profusely, and she smiled and said, "Not at all, we are completely at your service." The mice stirred again at this, and seemed to be trying to escape from the blouse.

None the less, Boris practically forgot her in the next few days as he waited each morning for the mail. When the package finally came he tore off the outer brown paper and the gift-wrapping in a single layer like a bridegroom on a wedding-night in his impatience to get at the contents. "My friend has sent me some cologne," he told himself. And it was Narcisse, the most expensive brand. A small bottle, it was true, but it was the thought that mattered and his friend wasn't rich. With a deep pleasure he went into the bathroom, took off his shirt, and touched his cologne-moistened fingers to the small fringe of hair at the center of his chest. An odor of musk and Greek islands filled the small tiled cubicle. He smiled. There as a little scar on his face below and to the left of his mouth, almost healed now. His friend watched him, content.

"Dear friend," he wrote on a piece of paper (it was the last piece in the desk and a little soiled now), "I have to write you a very special letter and ask you something I haven't asked before. You can refuse if you like. Will you meet me somewhere? It would give me pleasure if you did. Although who knows how it will change our friendship. Perhaps for the better, perhaps not. I will be at the Metropole Gaiety Hotel, by the Pier-glass, Wednesday at three o'clock. I enclose my photo so you will recognize me. Your friend, Boris."

He tore off the top one of the three remaining photographs, the one where he was only nervous and had not yet been dazzled by the flash, and put it in the letter and mailed it. But when the letter had disappeared in the box, and he had time to think it over in the silence of his apartment, he began to be assailed by doubts. What if his friend didn't come to the rendezvous? What if he came but didn't look at all like the photograph, or if he were ordinary instead of handsome? "What if he doesn't exist," the idea now occurred to Boris, "what if he exists only in my mind, if he is only something I have thought of?" Because, in his heart of hearts, he had to admit that the proof of the letters was not very convincing. And yet, now that this doubt had arisen, there was no way to allay it except to go to the rendezvous itself, as anxious and uncertain as this prospect now made him.

If his friend didn't come, of course, it might be not because he didn't exist but for some other reason—perhaps because his declaration of friendship had been insincere and he actually had other friends he preferred, friends he met every day instead of merely writing letters to. He might even have a girl, someone for instance like the clerk at the For Monsieur stand. In which case he and she, with her dark mysterious eyes and her smile, might read over Boris' letters together and laugh at them, treating the whole business of Boris as a joke (because she would tell him, of course, about the cologne).

As he thought about this Boris became more deeply anxious than he had ever been before, and quite unhappy. He went into the kitchen and listlessly pulled open various drawers and cupboards for a while, until finally he found the revolver in the drawer with the tools and bits of string. It was perhaps not called a revolver at all but only a pistol, since there was nothing on it to revolve, and it was only an L-shaped contrivance of metal with a tube sticking out one end, and the lever hanging down below around which the finger fitted nicely. He put this in his pocket and began looking for the bullet. It wasn't in the drawer, even though he took everything out of it and laid the contents on the sink, shaking the drawer upside down afterwards. He was certain there was a bullet somewhere in the apartment, but although the place was small there were a surprising number of drawers, cupboards, and closets in it where the bullet might be hiding. Finally he found it, in the bottom drawer of the desk in a box where he kept things like paper-clips. It was surprisingly small and the brass part of it was rather tarnished; clearly it needed oiling. He embarked on another systematic search of the apartment, this time looking for a small can of oil of the kind sold for use with typewriters. This was absolutely not to be found, and besides he was losing his patience. He went into the kitchen and put some olive oil on the bullet. After he had polished it with a rag it glowed quite nicely, with a patina to it like that of bronze statues in museums. He slipped it into the little hole at the rear of the pistol; it fitted perfectly and the mechanism closed over it with a click. He took a deep breath. He still didn't feel very good.

On Wednesday, putting the pistol in his pocket and taking the photograph with him from the mirror, he set off for the Metropole Gaiety Hotel. He had started early, and he went around a long way through back streets in order to use up more time. When the imposing baroque facade of the hotel was in front of him it was still a few minutes before three. It was important not to arrive too early and give his friend the impression that he was too eager, or that he had nothing else to do but come to appointments with him. It would be better to go in exactly at three, or better yet at one minute after three. He felt against his wrist the trotting of the little needle that ate up the seconds one by one. But he forced himself not to look at his watch, since if his friend happened to come along the sidewalk just at that moment he might take it as another evidence of anxiety or eagerness on his part.

When he finally looked at the watch it was four minutes past three; the moving hand had almost reached five. In a small panic at the idea of being late, he hurried in through the heavy glass door. But he was just in time; he caught sight of his friend, reflected in the pier-glass, approaching from a diagonal direction. So he had come! Boris was filled with a warm and reassuring happiness. He had no difficulty recognizing him; the narrow, slightly furtive face was exactly like the one in the photograph. His friend even had his own habit of glancing to one side rather than to the front as he walked across a room, and like Boris he carried one hand in his coat-pocket. (It was the left hand and not the right, but even this complementary symmetry seemed significant to Boris and pleased him more than a total identity).

He stopped, and his friend did too, smiling faintly. It struck him that there was something unsatisfactory about this practically total resemblance of his friend to himself, a resemblance he had already noticed in the photograph but which was now borne in upon him in its full force. The idea that began to form in his mind was that a friend is not a real friend if he is not different in some respect. His thoughts ran more or less thus: "If this is the way it is to be, if there is no difference between us and we are not strangers any more, then there is no point in our being friends, and it would be better if we didn't exist."

Reasoning thus, he took the pistol from his pocket, raised it, and applied it in slow motion to the side of his head, content to observe in the same moment that his friend was following his example. As he raised the pistol to his own temple his friend was watching him fixedly with a placid smile, the mouth raised a little higher on one side than on the other. Boris began to ponder this assymetry. When a person smiled with only one side of his mouth it was as though someone had told a joke that was only partly funny and not worth smiling totally about, or as though he knew a joke that somebody else didn't. Boris detected, now, a suggestion of something faintly mocking in this smile. And he began to suspect what it was. The conviction grew in him that his friend hadn't been entirely sincere in his declaration of friendship, or not sincere at all. It wasn't that he had other friends, but—Boris knew this now almost with a certainty—that he knew the girl at the For Monsieur stand, that he and she read his letters together and secretly laughed at Boris, not only because he didn't have a girl but because he didn't even have a friend, since his friend's declaration of friendship for him had been insincere.

He would have to act quickly, or his friend (he had no other term to apply to him even now that he was aware of his duplicity) would see what he was doing and try to do it first himself. With a single motion he removed the pistol from his head, turned it toward his friend, and pulled the little lever. There was a sharp report, far louder than he had imagined; it was as though someone had put a little chisel in his ear and struck it a sharp blow with a hammer. His friend smiled again, although this time it wasn't a real smile but a simulacrum caused by the disintegration of his face. Little lines ran outward in all directions on it, exactly like those caused by a smile. This mirth, in fact, extended to his whole person. Through a little cloud of smoke that hung in front of his still extended arm Boris saw his friend crack, splinter, crumple, and fall to the floor like a shower of silver fireworks. His smile was not visible at all now and parts of his body were missing. After a considerable pause (Boris was still holding the pistol outstretched for some reason) a piece of him the size of a hand fell onto the thick burgundy carpet and lay there glittering like ice. Boris himself was unharmed; if his friend had fired he had missed him, or it had been a second too late. The hotel manager came hurrying up. "What on earth do you think you're doing?" A deep depression had fallen over Boris. He handed the manager his friend's photograph. "This should be reported to the police," he muttered.

THE FUN DOME

Proctor's office was on Spring Street, and they had to walk down to Main and then cross over several blocks. They went at a rather slow pace because of Proctor's limp, if that is what it was. It would be more precise to say that he walked as though one of his feet was tender, although it was difficult to say which, the left or the right. Main Street gradually became more tawdry and at the same time more elaborate and colorful in a rather naive way. The signs on the stores were hand-painted in garish letters. They passed an herb-store specialising in Indian love-remedies, and another offering second-hand artificial legs and arms.

Proctor kept up a kind of impulsive and meandering monologue, in his high-pitched falsetto with its slight tremor, especially when he was on the point of laughter he was trying to repress. "You think you have problems. I had a patient once who tried to have an affair with a chicken. But it seems the chicken was a moralist. He came to me in a frenzy of unrequited love—it was Dantesque." In spite of himself he broke into silent laughter. "I could mention many such cases. Your own is unique, perhaps, only in its poetic tendencies, its power of vital synthesis so to speak. I have a lot of friends, but the people who really interest me tend to be masturbators—don't be offended," he put in quickly. "What do I mean by that? I mean simply that they are people whose physical life is richly controlled by their mental life, their imaginations. People who are capable of poetry, not the dull stuff they teach in schools, but *la poésie de la chaire . . .*"

He was really serious now. His mouth worked, especially on the French words, and his gestures were vehement and Shelleyian. In spite of the warm sunshine he was elegantly clad in a waistcoat and hound's tooth jacket, and a veil of perspiration was beginning to appear on his forehead.

"Let me put it another way," he continued, pushing back a lock from his pale forehead. "Life is short, baffling, and monotonous and as originally invented by God is rather mathematical. The planets move in their orbs, there are ten commandments and so forth. Monogamy, Kepler's third law, and the constitutions of modern plutodemocracies are all part of this pattern. Luckily man differs from the planets in having an imagination, that is in being capable of disobedience. Angels, on the other hand, don't have free will, and it is quite possible that the Revolt in Heaven was caused by boredom, so to speak. Now what can we do about this? Use our imaginations, spread sweetness and joy, and devise as many different kinds of yumyum as possible. Just now, for example, I'm on my way to meet a wonderful child named Bonnie Jean. Thirteen; tells her parents she's going to Christian Endeavor. Blond hair to the waist and lingerie from Sears. So innocent she agrees cheerfully to everything. Possibly, even probably, she might bring a friend."

"I'm not sure it sounds like my type."

"Ah, you have a type? What is it then?"

He felt a stupid color coming into his face. He didn't reply because he didn't know what kind of a girl was his type. That was his problem, and that was what Proctor was supposed to help him with. He felt a slight twinge of annoyance, which he managed to repress. Proctor didn't seem to notice. He had his hands clasped behind him and was gazing animatedly into the passing store-fronts with a little silent whistle. "Well, here we are," he said abruptly.

They had come to a large pile of domes, minarets, spires, trestled facades, and castellations built of cheap wood and painted a motley of flashy colors dominated by silver and gold. It filled the whole block on Main between Twentieth and Twenty-First. Over the main entrance was a filagreed arch with the word "Vendôme" in silver letters. Proctor went through the arch with his slightly swooping gait, and Caspian followed. Inside they came first into the Musée Mécanique, a large high-ceilinged room full of somewhat old-fashioned amusement machines. There were the usual electric rifles, peep-shows in which you turn the handle to make the cards flap around, and fortune-telling machines, along with a number of glass cabinets containing games or dolls manipulated by levers from the outside. He caught sight of one called "The Wedding Night" and another "The Shiek" (sic) "of Araby."

"There are the girls."

They were so small, and made up so inexpertly, that at first he took them for a pair of plaster dolls you win by throwing baseballs at bottles. Bobbie Jean had long blond hair, a round face, two porcelain eyes, and a cotton print dress that seemed too small for her. Cherry's hair was carrot-colored with a complexion to match. Both of them wore patent-leather shoes and socks turned down over their ankles. Bonnie Jean was chewing something, staring straight at Caspian. A tiny pink balloon appeared between her lips, expanded like a rapidly growing tumor, and exploded with a moist pop. She giggled when this made him start. There was a not unpleasant odor of cinnamon. Expertly she chewed the ruined balloon back into her mouth.

"I brought Cherry."

"I see you did."

"You brought somebody too."

"As you see."

"Gee, you're funny."

"No, I'm Doc, you're funny."

"No, you're crazy, I'm Bonnie."

This sophisticated repartée seemed really to amuse her. The repressed laughter inside her was like a kind of pressurized soda-water, bubbling constantly at her eyes and the corners of her mouth. Now and then it spurted out in little snorts. Proctor took her by one arm and Cherry by the other and pulled them away, Caspian trailing along.

Cherry wanted to try the electric rifle. "You can shoot the President or the Pope or anybody. Last week I shot Gandhi, whoever he is."

"No, that's dumb."

Instead they stopped at the Syco-Anal-Isis machine. Proctor supplied the coins for everybody. There were only about a dozen levers so the number of questions you could ask was limited. Proctor pushed a lever labeled *Does Chloé love me?* and a small doll in a frock-coat and Van Dyke bent jerkily over, opened the cabinet, and held up a sign saying *To understand women too well throws some doubt on your verility.*

Caspian tried. The levers marked "Why was I born?" and "When will I die?" didn't interest him. He selected, "Why am I unhappy?" The Viennese doctor bent over, opened the cabinet, and came up with a tiny sign (all of them were misspelled): "One of God's oversights. You can't attend to everything in a busness as large as his." There were other answers for everybody. "Is Jack faithful to me?" "Ingorance is bliss." "Why do I dream at night?" "You've got to think somtime."

"Oh come on. This is even dumber than shooting the Pope."

Bonnie pulled them away toward "The Wolf Hunt." It consisted of a glass cabinet with a plaster landscape in it and two metal dolls: a Neanderthal with a cloak and a spear, and a small gray wolf with the paint worn off his back in places.

"Doc! Doc, give us the money."

She and Cherry got on opposite sides of the cabinet and worked the levers. There were seven or eight of them on each side; it was quite complicated. Some made the figures go back and forth, others turned, one worked the spear, and so on. The wolf ran around in various slots in the plaster landscape, turned on its tail, and tried to bite the man in the ankle. But Cherry adroitly lifted the Neanderthal's leg out of the way, turned him around in a U-shaped slot to approach the wolf from the rear, and stuck the spear in the wolf just under his foreleg. The wolf made a yelp and a tiny thread of red came from his mouth. He lay on his back, all four legs in the air.

Bonnie sulked. "The Neanderthal always wins. I get to be the Neanderthal next time."

"You *wanted* to be the wolf. You always take the wolf. You always think you can make him win, but you can't."

Proctor smoothed it over. "Let's try 'Romans and Sabines.' That way everybody can play."

"Oh goodie! That's my favorite."

Proctor produced the coins again and they took up their positions. There were at least twenty dolls inside the glass case, and four times as many levers on the outside. The décor was classic, with ruined temples, corinthian pillars, and even a hanging garden. The Sabine ladies were clad in tiny real gowns, slit along one side so that they flopped open when the dolls turned sharp corners. The Romans were naked except for armor over their chests, as in the famous painting by David. Caspian worked a Sabine with his left hand and a Roman with his right. He wasn't sure what he was trying to do. If you worked a Roman the point was to chase a Sabine around and try to corner her against a column or under the hanging garden. Then you could make him fall onto her and mount her, or pierce her with his short sword; or you could do both at once if you were dexterous. But this took at least three hands (it seemed to Caspian) and his left hand was occupied with the Sabine woman he had somehow taken on without quite wishing to accept this responsibility. His Sabine was being pursued by a Roman manipulated by Cherry, and meanwhile he was trying to trap Proctor's Sabine with his own Roman. The figures ran around in their little slots in fascinating confusion. Bonnie's trick was to let her Sabine be almost captured by a Roman and then twist the doll around so that it fell on its stomach instead of its back. The Roman didn't know what to do. (That is, the person manipulating him didn't; the game carried you away so that you almost forgot). To cover her in that posture would be undignified, so in most cases he stuck his sword in the part of her presented. When this happened a little red spurt appeared, just as in the wolf speared by the Neanderthal.

But Proctor, when his Roman cornered her Sabine, was not thwarted by this maneuver. He got the Roman's sword under the female doll and started trying to pry her over onto her back. Bonnie countered, trying to make the Sabine crawl along on all fours into the shelter of a ruined temple. But she made a wrong turn and Proctor got her up a cul-de-sac where the slot came to an end. She furiously manipulated her levers and he his. It was like playing a complicated organ; their fingers flew from one lever to another. Once the Roman succeeded in turning the Sabine over, but she flopped back onto her stomach again. The Roman got the sword under her and twisted. Over she went again, and the Roman wasted no time in falling onto her. Both figures shuddered, in a series of little jerks like the clapper of a doorbell.

"Oh, *you*." She was really exasperated. Evidently Proctor always won. Cherry was having somewhat better luck. Her Sabine had successfully eluded all Romans and was parading tauntingly along the top of the garden. Caspian began pursuing her more vigorously, turning both hands to the task and abandoning his own Sabine which nobody was chasing now anyhow. He maneuvered his Roman up to the top of the garden and cornered Cherry's Sabine in a kind of a niche, a hemispherical concavity of architecture. The slots in the niche were shaped like an H; there were two positions for the Roman and two for the Sabine. Whenever he went to the right the female doll slid to the left, and vice versa. It was like the predicament in checkers where you trap your opponent's last piece in the corner; he can move back and forth indefinitely while you wear yourself out trying to follow him. The thing was to be quicker than Cherry in moving the levers, but she had more practice. Her fingers were nimble; the doll sprang back and forth so vigorously that its feminine charms were constantly exposed by the flying gown. The Roman turned to follow her, always a half-second late. Finally a little white spurt came from between his legs and arched onto the plaster ground. The levers were jammed. The Roman wouldn't move any more.

"Old Jack Praecox, my favorite Roman," giggled Cherry. The game was over; Proctor and Bonnie had finished too. The machine wouldn't work any more until more coins were put in. They went on to some others. "Perseus and Andromeda" was fairly interesting. The maiden, a facsimile of the well-known figure by Ingres, was chained to a rock and an unlikely monster was about to devour her. Up came the knight wearing a helmet and a jacket of chain-mail over his chest. He had two weapons, a spear and a sword, for attacking the monster. But this game allowed for only three players, one for each of the characters, and the player who had Andromeda could do little except make her writhe. Caspian, who played Perseus, finally slew the dragon by spearing it just under its cat-like whiskers. Next came "The Wedding Night." This was for two players only. Bonnie and Proctor tried it. The décor was Victorian and the costumes to match. The bridegroom tried to disrobe the bride, using little hooks on the ends of his hands. There were many petticoats. Meanwhile the player operating the bride defended her as best he could, taking shelter behind the furniture and trying to scratch the bridegroom with little up-and-down motions of the arms. This might have been thought an uneven contest. But Bonnie, her barely suppressed giggles coming out now and then in a little spasm at the corners of her mouth, made her doll kick the groom deftly in the groin, disabling him so that the game was over.

"That's not fair."

"All's fair in love! And war!"

"Which is this?"

"Both!" shrieked the girls in unison. They were greatly enjoying themselves.

"What next?"

"The Oh machine. You get in it and the other person tries to make you say Oh."

"If you mean *I* get in it, no I don't."

"Then Trams of the World."

They went to Trams of the World. It was nothing but a kind of long metal box with rows of windows along the sides and a door at the rear. Inside there were benches. They sat down. "Not there," the girls told Caspian. "That's where the *passenger* sits." His mistake sent them into giggles again. Proctor went up to the front and remained standing, next to a pedestal with a rotating lever on it.

There were colored lights overhead in the ceiling. When Proctor put a coin in the pedestal and turned the rheostat these came on. There was a burring and clicking noise from underneath, and a kind of stereopticon formed in the windows. You could see snowy streets, onion-shaped steeples, and people in fur hats going by. The people had a jerky puppet-like way of moving and their features might have been chopped out with an axe. Across from Caspian, in the place where the girls had told him not to sit, the beams of light formed a figure in a great fur coat, a black beard, and a fur hat. It was rather badly done. You could see through parts of his elbow, and as the tram jerked the light didn't quite focus properly and pieces of his anatomy flowed out sideways like melting ice or developed large holes.

The girls conferred, tittering. Cherry asked him, "Ninochka pochka blotsky twotsky?"

"Nyet." But this deep basso was a piece of ventriloquism by Proctor, who had his back to them and his hand on the rheostat. It was rewarded with sputters of laughter.

As Proctor went on turning the rheostat the scene constantly changed. Some marble columns went by, and a pair of caryatids with broken noses holding up a temple. A sign on a shop said *MAKAPONI*. The passenger was a goddess with one breast bare and a quiver on her back. She had hardly any face at all; it was like a mask with black holes for the eyes and mouth. A click of the rheostat produced an oriental scene. Coolies went by carrying baskets, there was a temple with curled-up eaves, and so on. It seemed that here too there was a game the girls always played. Bonnie leaped over onto the passenger's seat just as Proctor turned the rheostat, and the oriental gentleman in his silk gown sat down on top of her. The flesh-and-blood creature and the statue of light struggled for some time, the oriental in silence and Bonnie with little shrieks and giggles. Finally he won and sat in dignified silence, his arm wavering a little as the lamp overhead wiggled. Bonnie came back and sat in her proper place. "Oh you," Cherry told her. "You should have grabbed his. You know."

"Pigtail!" More stifled puffs, exploding finally as their glances met.

Proctor moved the lever to the last position. They were going down Rue de Rivoli. An equestrian statue went by, then the Palais Royal and the Grand Magasin du Louvre. A sidewalk café with people drinking absinthe. In the seat opposite, under a sign reading, "Les places numérotées sont réservées aux femmes enceintes et aux mutilés de guerre," was a gentleman with a little pointed beard and waxed mustaches. He had a top hat and striped pants, and the rosette of the Légion d'Honneur in his buttonhole. He was reading *Le Monde*, but it was all very crude; you could barely make out the name of the newspaper.

"Vooley vooley vooley voo, m'sewer?"

"Fille de putain! Ta gueule! Fiche-moi la paix!"

The falsetto was skillful but the accent bad. Proctor had not even turned his head. The girls tittered uncontrollably like tickled babies. The tram slewed sideways, past a baroque façade and a square with an obelisk in it, and descended into a hole in the ground marked "Métropolitain." It was dark for some time. When the lights came on again the ride was over and they got out of the tram. After a moment of disorientation Caspian saw that they seemed to have arrived at some other part of the building. The Syco-Anal-Isis machine and the doll-cabinets were nowhere in sight. They went through an arch marked "To the Roller Palace," with a cluster of tin acanthus leaves over it and a chromograph of lovers holding hands. This led to a corridor with a somewhat undulating floor and then into a room with a domed ceiling, filled with a dazzling and kaleidoscopic mixture of light and sound.

It was slightly bewildering. Portions of the walls made of garishly painted plywood rotated or undulated in time to the music as the lights played on them. The floor was shaped like a shallow dish; it rotated too but in the direction opposite to the walls. In the middle of the floor, at the very geometric center of the room, was a large Whirlitzer the size of a small house, so brilliantly illuminated that it seemed to be made out of colored light. From this came a clangy and confident music that sounded as though it was made by pots and pans, pieces of sewer pipe, locomotive whistles, and exotic oriental harps.

Sitting down at the bench on one side, they put on their skates. Then they launched out onto the concave and gently swooping floor. There were a half-dozen or so other skaters on the floor going around counterclockwise at a rather alarming speed. But once out on the floor Caspian found it was easier than it seemed. The very velocity of the others, somehow, carried you along in their path. And there was no difficulty about turning corners because the shape of the floor took care of that. Curving around continually to the left was natural; it was going in a straight line that would have been difficult. Imitating what Proctor was doing with Bonnie, he grabbed Cherry from behind and swooped around moving his legs in unison with hers. This brought the center of his body, at each stride, almost underneath her childish bottom that was shaped like two neat and perfectly round tennis balls and not much larger. But since she was so small bringing himself into this position required a low swoop, almost a dip, with every motion of his legs, and this gave him an undulating and birdlike motion that was not only fatiguing but must have seemed ludicrous to the spectators. No one else was doing this. Convinced that he was supposed to roll around in some way united with Cherry, he tried putting himself in front of her, facing the same way, and fastening her hands onto his waist. After some giggling she understood what he had in mind. They flew around the circle in this manner for a few turns. But he couldn't any longer see her or even feel her, except for the light grip of her hands under his ribs, which tickled a little. The music blared on, with the enthusiasm of a military band strayed somehow into a erotic mood. A tinny voice, evidently made by the same machine, was now singing.

> Come to me my artificial baby
> Close your eyes and paint your toenails blue

He was getting the hang of the skates and had more confidence now. Turning adroitly on one skate while still in motion, he placed himself face-to-face with Cherry and seized her waist in this position. She laughed and put her own hands a little lower on his body, at the level of the hips. This was better. He could see her and as a couple they had more control because they were both holding onto each other.

> All your tears are in my fancy maybe
> You know dear what I will do to you

But there was a disadvantage. Either he was going backwards or she was. Since neither liked to do this, it turned into a kind of pirouetting contest in which first he was moving backwards, then she, then he, then she. He was stronger, but she was agile and had more practice at the business. Finding himself going backwards, he would tighten his grip on her waist, give a wrench, and rotate rapidly so that he was going forward again, pushing her stern first around the circular floor. But this configuration was unstable. It was like trying to make a boat go by pushing it from behind with a pole. The slightest error in steering and she would slew off to one side, cleverly using her weight so that he found himself whirled around into backward position again.

I know dear that you'll be bound to please me
All my dreams will then come true

In this process, he began to notice now, he and Cherry had gradually worked themselves farther and farther from the center of this Dantesque whirlwind and almost out to the edge of the floor. As they did this their velocity decreased until it almost came to a stop. For the first time now he began to see the whole point of the game of skating. The thing was to work yourself continually inward as you circled, closer and closer to the Whirlitzer at the center of the floor. As you did this, by a well-known law of physics your velocity increased, and at the same time the added centrifugal force made it harder and harder to work toward the center. Strenuous effort was required, along with considerable skill. He and Cherry stopped with their hands on the railing and watched Proctor and Bonnie do it. They were almost at the Whirlitzer now and the centrifugal force pushed them outward like a powerful hand. None of the other skaters had managed to get nearly as close to the center. Now they were only a foot or two from the low railing that separated the Whirlitzer from the rotating floor. Here the centrifugal force was terrific. They lost a little and had to begin working their way inward again. Caspian could see Proctor's silent laugh; he even took one hand from Bonnie's waist to brush the hair from his forehead. Now he was almost there; he had made it and he and Bonnie leaped over the low railing with the skates still on their feet. In an instant they were inside the little house of the Whirlitzer.

After that they were visible only intermittently. Now and then Caspian caught a glimpse of them floating by a window, Proctor with his Wagnerian hero's erection, his little smile and his froglike hands, Bonnie still giggling although nothing could be heard over the din, the jangly music playing over their naked shoulders, their limbs, the garments that fell from them one by one like leaves in autumn.

So come my funny dear
While I lash away each tear
Or else I shall be artificial too

Caspian and Cherry clambered over the railing, sat down on a bench, and took off their skates. She seemed not at all disconcerted that they hadn't made it to the center of the floor. It was not even entirely clear that she understood this was the point of the game. Perhaps for her it wasn't. Her hair was disarrayed; there were points of perspiration on her carrot-colored neck. He set about trying to make light conversation with her and it went fairly well.

"I like your name."

"It means dear in French."

"Is that so?"

"I just love the Fun Dome, don't you?"
"Do you come here very often?"
"Oh, I never leave the place. I practically live here."
"What game do you like best?"
"I know what *you* like best," she countered.
"What?"
"I know." Her mouth-corners quivered and her nose began making little snuffs of amusement. "You know, I like you."

Caspain noticed now that she had ink-stains on her fingers and had written her name on the back of one hand in India ink. On the other hand was a heart and somebody's initials. She smelled of strawberry candy, of perspiration, and of talcum. The last was exactly the smell you made when the teacher had you knock two erasers together to get the chalk off them. It went not unpleasantly with the odor of perspiration—not real sweat but baby-sweat—and the faint aroma of strawberry jam. He got up to take his leave of her.

"Au revoir. And thanks for all the innuendoes."

She giggled. "You know, you're really *funny*." She raised her hand to the level of her shoulder and bent the fingers down.

"Bye bye."

Then a thing occurred that happens frequently when parting from people. You make your farewells, start off in a certain direction, and then find the other person is going the same way too. He had intended to go back into the Musée Mécanique and then out the main entrance of the building, the way he had come in. But Cherry was going that way too. After some misunderstanding and a feint or two (a final giggle from Cherry) he reversed himself and went off the other way, around the Roller Dome and out a side door. Unexpectedly this brought him out on Twentieth Street, around the corner from Main. To his surprise the sun had set and the air was graying. The shop-signs were beginning to come on one after the other, making small red and green wounds in the evening gloom. It took him a long time to walk back to the lot at Fourth and Spring where he had left his car. He would have to get a better analyst, he decided. It was a mistake having your friend for a doctor.

THE DOG MAFIA

My discovery that the dogs of the world are able to communicate among themselves arose, in the first place, from particular circumstances in my own life and my relation to canine society. Like many other discoveries in the history of science it did not come suddenly but grew from the gradual and almost imperceptible accumulation of data from various quarters. I have never been a dog owner nor am I what is commonly termed a dog lover. My first personal contact with the world of dogs took place a few years ago when, because of circumstances that are too complicated to explain here and besides not pertinent to the matter under discussion, I found myself in Paris and in a particular and quite special frame of mind or, more precisely, *état d'âme*. But why conceal that my difficulties involved the opposite sex, an interlude in my life which I would prefer to conceal but which will inevitably come to light? Briefly, I was caught in the grip of forces over which I have no control, forces which ended by producing in me a residue of unresolved hostility which I discharged, I am sorry to say, on the dogs I happened to encounter in the street. I would entice them to me through the simple devices traditional in man-dog relations and then, when they were in suitable proximity, I would deal them shrewd kicks in the manner made famous and even, I believe, invented by Charlie Chaplin: to wit, if the dog approaches from the left, the right foot is crossed behind the left calf and a sharp jab dealt using the left calf as interference or a kind of shield, so to speak, out of which the toe darts like the tongue of a serpent and then retreats quickly to its normal position; or, should the approach of the dog occur from the right, the identical technique with coordinates reversed. If this is done properly the process is practically too fast for the eye to follow. The casual observer only a few yards away will fail to perceive the shoe that flashes out from behind the trouser-leg and will notice only that the dog, for some inexplicable reason, has terminated his approach at a range of perhaps eighteen inches and is withdrawing rapidly, and as inconspicuously as possible, from the scene of action. You will notice I do not refer to howls, yelps, or audible complaints of any kind. The dogs of Paris, at least the ones I happened to encounter, were much too hardened by their experience of urban life to reveal their emotions in any such obvious way. After a momentary muscular reflex, the kind of contraction made by a sea-anemone when pressed with the finger, they took themselves off rapidly without so much as a glance behind them at the person who had reacted so unexpectedly and treacherously to their overtures. They knew the world and they were pragmatists; they saw no point in empty rhetoric which could do nothing to remedy the injustice which, in any case, they accepted as a normal condition or axiom of their existence.

It is not my purpose to attempt to justify my own moral behavior in these incidents, even if there were any moral grounds on which to make such a defense; and in any case the circumstances, in our universe, often have a way of providing their own solution to a moral imbalance. Let it suffice to say that more recently, after I returned to my own country, I began to perceive the first hints of some causative connection between my own previous behavior vis-à-vis the Paris dogs and the common attitude toward me which I detected in the dogs of the city in which I found myself living. By this time my personal circumstances were greatly changed. In Paris I had been relatively affluent; now I was poor. In Paris I had been full of hostility and violence, now I have reached a condition of inward peace, or at least of the equilibrium of neuroses (unhappinesses). There I had lived in society and experienced violent emotions in my relations with others; here I lived in a vacuum and suffered from loneliness. In short I was another person, or imagined that I was, and in this new guise or identity I began to take an interest in the behavior of the dogs I began to notice in extraordinary numbers in the streets. In this somewhat provincial city (a state capital, but of a rather backward state) the men seemed apathetic and moved about listlessly in what appeared to be a purposeless way, and indeed I myself could harldy see any purpose in transferring one's self to any particular part of this city in preference to any other part. But the dogs seemed to trot along toward unknown destinations with a real sense of purpose. They made their way directly down sidewalks, turned corners at right angles, and unfailingly found alleys, paths, and missing boards in fences according to some hidden plan. This interested me, and since I had nothing else to do anyhow I began observing this behavior more closely. As a start I began following individual dogs across the city, or attempting to. I remember that the first dog I tried to follow was a rather nondescript terrier the color of a felt hat, and he behaved exactly like all the others. For a while he comported himself in a conventional doglike way, trotting along with a glance now and then at interesting objects on one side or the other, a brief pause to water a pole and check for messages, a diagonal crossing of a boulevard with a cautious eye out for trucks. But soon I began to perceive, or sense in some subliminal way, that the dog was not behaving in a normal way, instead that he was aware I was observing him and was behaving in what I as a human being expected and thought of as conventional doglike behavior. And, at the same time, something in his performance suggested that he wished to communicate the falseness of this simulacrum to me in some elusive way that I could not overtly charge him with — that there was an irony in his manner that was directed unmistakably toward me even though he had shown no formal awareness of my presence or existence. The climax of the incident left no doubt about the matter. When I went toward him he stood motionlessly and stoically, almost indifferently, between two trash-cans and watched me approach. I knelt, a traditional gesture in man-dog relations signifying symbolically that I wished to put myself on his level. (There is no need to point out the condescension implied in this.) Then I held out my hand and made conciliatory sounds. Come here, boy. Hey. Howsa dog. Hi there, fella. Come on, now. Come here. The result was a startling one, and one I can describe only in anthropomorphic terms. He remained motionless for another moment or two, and then he smiled: I mean the lip rose a little on one side, revealing his teeth. His expression was one of a knowing and ironic contemptuousness. Then he simply turned and walked away. He had not snapped, or growled, or "bared his teeth," or done anything conventionally doglike. There was no question about it, what I had seen was a totally controlled and ironic smile (I might almost have said a "human" smile except that this adjective was rapidly ceasing to have any meaning), the irony of which was unmistakably directed at me.

Decidedly the situation was more complex than I had imagined. The whole matter demanded a more formal and thorough investigation than it had heretofore been given if I was to get at the bottom of it. In the several weeks that followed it became clear to me that there was something—not "unnatural," perhaps, but at least curious and hitherto unperceived—in the behavior of the dogs of this city. Their doglike antics, their peeing, chasing after trucks, quarreling and sparring amng themselves, biting and shaking inedible objects, was an elaborate hoax intended to cover up their real interests and activities. And their behavior toward me—their droping of this farcical manner in certain instants of private and intimate confrontation—clearly indicated their own knowledge of my behavior toward the dogs of Paris. The dogs of the world communicated among one another.

It seemed to me that my first step, in investigating the manner and content of this communication, was to examine the general matter of dogs and language. Now everyone knows the folklore of dog-lovers in this respect. Every dog owner repeats, "That dog understands every word I say to him." And he can even cite evidence to back up his assertion: that the dog when so ordered will run out to the sidewalk and bring back the newspaper, that he comprehends and reacts appropriately to simple terms like "dinner," "bad dog," "fetch," and "How about going for a walk, old fellow?" According to this same folklore, dogs can even formulate sounds crudely paralleling human speech: croons, yelps of agreement, ashamed whimpers. Even for a non-dog-lover it is easy to see that, after a certain degree of prolonged intimacy with a given dog, a human being may establish a kind of communication along these lines which may even be termed "verbal" to some degree. But what I am concerned with is not this sort of interspecial pidgin but another form of language in dogs which I eventually came to master intuitively even though to this day I am not quite sure of its mechanics. (It is not really a "language," since this word comes from *lingua*, tongue, and the tongue in dogs is not an organ of communication. Instead it serves as an organ of thermometric stability, the dog opening his mouth and panting across it when he is hot and closing his mouth again when he is cold. In humans this function is assumed by the epidermis, and incidentally one of the characteristics of humans that dogs find most disgusting is this business of perspiration or having tongue all over one's outside, an affront to the olfactory sense. Dogs do not use their skin in this way, or in fact for anything else except the obvious function of holding their insides together, although I would not exclude the possibility that the skin itself is the organ of speech in dogs. This would be a kind of symmetry in the phylogenetic network; it is known that sharks hear with their skin. As you can see I do not understand very well this thing I am supposed to be explaining. The important thing is that I have been able to master it well enough for practical purposes; and how many humans can explain to you the exact operation of the larynx?)

That dogs can speak is then a piece of accepted folklore. But what the average person—I dare say even the average dog-lover—will be less likely to admit is that dog language is capable of framing and expressing abstract concepts. Obviously "shame" is an abstract concept, and dogs can feel shame, communicate it, and detect it in others. But humans in general have an excessive respect for the sophistication and complexity of their language, a complexity they believe unique in the animal world. And yet my investigations—the first, I venture to say, ever made from a canine point of view and totally without anthropomorphizing—soon led me to the discovery that dog language could deal with any concept expressible in ordinary human speech, even of the most complicated kind. The error that had blocked other investigators was the belief that there is something uniquely human about abstract thought. In reality abstractions are simply thought-clusters assembled from two or more concretions. "Abnegation," for example, is formed by combining the ideas of "away" and "no." Every dog-lover would affirm that his dog understands "away" and "no." But he denies, for some reason, that the dog is capable of grasping "away-no-ness" or abnegation. Thus a dog may say in clear terms comprehensible even to a human, "I abnegate dinner," i.e. "No, I am angry with you, I will not eat my dinner, take it away." Likewise "consideration" (together we look at the stars), "companionship" (a thing in which we eat bread together), and "immaculate conception" (a no-dirt way of making puppies). Please note that I don't say dogs *believe* in immaculate conception, only that they are able to grasp the concept. As a matter of fact when I first explained this term to dogs I was greeted with polite laughter.

In short, there is no point in my describing the techniques through which, in months of painstaking effort, I succeeded in establishing communication with dogs on their own terms, that is, in the framework of their own expressive and conceptualizing system rather than my own. The examples I have given above can offer only a very crude idea of the differences between canine and human speech and the effort of the intellect necessary to bridge this chasm. Let it suffice to say that in time I achieved this and was accepted by the dogs, at least in a limited respect, as one of themselves. It was a long time before they got over their suspicion of me, and indeed I myself was obliged to recognize that I bore a weight of culpability toward their species that could be removed only through continued evidence of good faith on my part. I will not say that I "won their confidence"—they are too astute to be taken in by efforts to "win their confidence"—or even that I "convinced them of my sincerity." There is no question of sincerity or insincerity in canine language, which unlike human speech is designed to express the thoughts of the speaker rather than conceal them. I simply worked, learned, and at last understood, and when I understood I became *ex causa* and through this itself a practical member of the species.

One of the first things I discovered when I reached this plane of knowledge is that the alleged faithfulness of dogs is an enormous and conspiratorial sham. I had many conversations on this subject with Epworth, a Newfoundland I met in a public park. Dogs simulate fidelity because it serves their own ends. If cats do not, it is not because they have different ends but because they have elected different means to achieve these ends. Epworth—and again this is a discovery which would shock a dog-lover—had more respect for cats than for people. People pretend to love dogs and understand them, but in reality there is an ineradicable basis of condescension in their attitude. ("Condescension" is easily broken down to its concretes: with + descend, you are below me, I come down to be with you.) The proof of this, according to Epworth, is that they have not permitted intermarriage. In fact intercourse between the species is so horrible a crime that it is punished in secret and not even discussed; many dog-lovers will deny its existence. It should be made clear that Epworth himself had no personal desire for intermarriage. He thought it was impractical, and was convinced that everybody concerned would be happier with their own kind. But these incidents do occur, and it would be foolish to deny them. Dogs will occasionally attempt amorosity with a knee or other protruding limb, simply out of a sense of experiment in order to see whether there is anything in the possibility. As everyone knows, such incidents cause embarrassment among humans and are quickly punished. These attempts, as ill-conceived as they may be, are at least candid and public. But Epworth contended that an even greater number of overtures take place in the opposite direction, in short that people lust after dogs far more frequently than dogs lust after people. Such incidents invariably take place in secret, but they are well known to dogs, who discuss them freely. Only very rarely are these aberrations detected, and then they result in an inflexible and terrible punishment. (The punishment proceeds entirely from the human side, it should be clear; whatever dogs may think about interspecial coitus, they are not convinced that the infliction of suffering is any answer to sin.) I explained the name applied by humans to this behavior: bestiality, "behaving like an animal." Epworth hardly even bothered to smile at this.

His point, however, was that in spite of the overwhelming evidence that humans lust after dogs, intermarriage is forbidden, and on grounds that are entirely irrational. It is no good arguing that such unions would be sterile; some of the greatest relationships in the history of love have remained without issue, from Heloise and Abelard to Bonnie and Clyde. Epworth reminded me that marriage can take place without offspring and offspring without marriage, so there is no point bringing the two into common consideration. (The notion that animals do not understand the relation between coitus and reproduction is one of the myths perpetuated by man to nourish his own superiority.) Besides no one doubts that humans, with their impressive biotechnology, could solve this problem if they put their minds to it for only a few weeks. In short, what it came down to was this. The dog-lover cherishes an image of dog as Man's Best Friend. Yes, but would you want your sister to marry one? Well, they wouldn't be happy, and besides it would be hard to find an apartment, and unfair to the children should there be any. Yes, we know the arguments.

As for old ladies and their lap-dogs, Epworth left this kind of thing to specialists. Let it suffice to say that if the old ladies are protected by their naivete the lap-dogs know perfectly well what it is all about. Why, then, do the lap-dogs generate such an elaborate simulacrum of enjoyment, gratitude, and suchlike emotions in response to the behavior in question? The investigation of this enigma led me far beyond erotic matters and into areas of vastly greater significance. Epworth, for all his intelligence and perspicuity, was a commonsensical fellow in the theory of history or in fundamental questions of any kind. Most of what I learned in these areas came to me from Von Rundstedt, a Weimaraner whom I met through a rather involved set of common friends, both human and canine. (Here I ought to acknowledge especially the assistance of Dorn, who not only showed a keen understanding of, and sympathy with, my somewhat unusual friendships but freely offered me the hospitality of his home, a generosity which made possible contacts of a social nature which would have been out of the question in the somewhat sterile institution where he served as a physician and where I was theoretically supposed to be confined.) Epworth and Von Rundstedt were as different as the average of two human beings you might happen to meet. Where Epworth had been pragmatic, Von Rundstedt was metaphysical in his inclinations and especially acute in the history of ideas. Through him I learned the history of his race—not systematically or in chronological order in the manner of a university lecture, but rather in bits and pieces, illustrations which he offered in support of abstract arguments, chance remarks which he dropped in the course of our conversations on a variety of topics, which only later I pieced together into their proper sequences. This history began not only with the origin of the species but with the beginnings of its systematic relations with man. In brief, the dog-race lacked any particular consciousness of its taxonomic identity until this sense arose out of reaction to genus Homo. At a certain point in history it became clear to the Canidae, or at least to certain of its thinkers and intellectual exponents, that the race of man was in a process of ascendency that would inevitably lead it to predominance over the animal world. There were those, incidentally, who did not accept this inevitablity—in fact at an early stage those who contended that man was destined to predominate were regarded as defeatists—but subsequent developments, particulary the development of fire and the fabrication of pointed weapons, made it clear to all but the most fanatic chauvinists that man's victory over the animal kingdom was inevitable. At this point, as so often happens in history, there was dissension and uncertainty in the ranks of the defeated. In general there were three opinions as to the action to be taken. A radical and nationalistic faction—the Lupine party, as it later became known—vowed a savage enmity to the race of man, a tactics of ferocity and banding together. A somewhat more moderate element, while equally uncompromising in its hostility to man, argued that open confrontation was impractical in view of the advantage, a temporary one at least, of the enemy. These Vulpines therefore advocated a policy of agility and flight: avoidance of confrontation, petty theft and harassment, guerrilla tactics. The third and most moderate faction (or as they preferred to define it, the most rational and far-sighted) argued for simulated fidelity, compromise, and temporal accommodation. That this last strategy succeeded the best is demonstrated by the fact that this party inherited the title of Canis or dog which previously had been shared by all. The wolves, in spite of a number of local and temporary victories which were negligible in their total effect, were soon crushed under the superior technology of the enemy. They were gradually forced into remote and inhospitable regions of the world and are today approaching extinction. The foxes fared little better. At first their tactics of furtiveness seemed to promise somewhat more success that the ferocity of the wolves, but the invention by man of more efficient hunting techniques—including the enlistment of certain tribes of the dogs themselves as reconnaissance and light attack groups against their former cousins—reduced them to a precarious existence of hiding in holes and hollow stumps. It was one of the ignominies of the foxes' fate, that, when their gradual defeat seemed to have brought them to the point of extinction, man was obliged to regulate their slaughter in order for a remnant of the race to survive for his sport. Even the wolves had not been obliged to taste this humiliation.

Meanwhile the Canines, in their policy of simulated surrender, succeeded beyond their wildest expectations. At man's behest they entered into his house, guarded his children and his hearth, ate the food he provided them, and even accommodated their reproductive habits to his whims in the matter of breeding. Even though any individual dog, at this stage in the process, was capable of seizing any individual man by the throat and destroying him, the dogs subdued their reflexes in this matter to the point where a folklore of their fidelity began to grow and propagate itself among mankind. While the wolves shivered in the snow and stole occasional sheep, while the foxes trembled in their holes, the dogs ate man's food and grew strong. Meanwhile they encouraged the notion of their character that man was only too ready to accept: simple and merry-minded slaves, eager to win their masters' approval and anxious above all to amuse. They accepted men's gestures of affection with a tail-wagging and general cringing that the wolves would have regarded as obscene if they had ever witnessed it, but the wolves did not witness it; they were far away freezing on the Carpathian snows. Among themselves men spoke of dog's fidelity, of his simple-minded affection for them, of how well the understood him, and of how fortunate dogs were to have surrendered their freedom in return for the advantages man was in a position to offer. Among themselves the dogs talked of—but what they talked of I discovered only relatively late in my investigations, when the dogs had ceased to regard me as a threat to the security of their plans, or more precisely had concluded that my situation among my fellow-men was such that they were not likely to believe the improbable fantasies I might contrive out of what would be regarded as a disordered imagination.

That dogs communicated among themselves over long distances, however, I suspected from the beginning, and I received further and unmistakable evidence of this as my investigations continued. Von Rundstedt constantly distinguished between his own opinion and those of his immediate friends—i.e. dogs he knew personally and saw every day—and the opinions of dogs in other lands and of different social circumstances. In the Orient, as he explained, where men were not quite as sentimental in their relations with dogs and regarded them more as a source of food than as companions, dogs had a lower opinion of their masters and hardly even regarded it as necessary to deceive them through tail-wagging and other simulations of cravenness. And in Mohammedan countries, where the whole race of dogs was considered unclean, the dogs scarcely disguised their enmity at all, and even on occasion banded together like wolves to attack men in lonely places where success seemed likely. I suggested to Von

Rundstedt that dogs' low opinion of men in these backward countries was connected to the relative crudeness of the civilization in such places, and that if there was a greater respect for man in western countries it was because man's material technology—the original reason for the dogs' policy of simulated surrender and accommodation—had reached its highest development in these areas. To my surprise Von Rundstedt was not very much impressed by the material development of our civilization. It was true that this development, through the invention of weapons for hunting and other warfare, had given man the ascendency over animals that had determined, out of negative reaction, the whole national philosophy of the Canines. But for this ascendency a stick pointed and hardened in the fire was sufficient; as soon as the crudest weapon was invented the dogs had been obliged to fall back on a strategy of non-confrontation, and in this regard they were put at no more disadvantage by the most sophisticated of weapons than they were by the sharpened stick. As for the rest of the technology we were so proud of—man's ability to duplicate functions performed by the buzzard, the porpoise, the meteorite, etc.—these seemed to him a kind of mimicry that might amuse the very young but was hardly of interest to mature minds. Like our cleverness in depilating our bodies which then necessitated clothing, clothing which in turn necessitated the invention of the washing machine, and so on. Oddly enough the one technical feat of man that impressed Von Rundstedt was the ability to open cans. It did not seem remarkable to him that man had learned to put foods in cans in the first place. It is not very difficult, he pointed out, to hide things so that they become inaccessible. As a matter of fact he could see no necessity for storing food, the proper place to store food was in one's stomach, but he was ready to let that pass. The fact was that an enormous quantity of food *was* stored in cans, he himself had no precise notion of the quantity and he doubted that men themselves had, but in any case it was surely enough to nourish the whole race of dogs for an unlimited time. The can-opener was a very simple device, but it had been contrived by men to accommodate to their own anatomy and its operation, at least for the present, lay beyond the ability and even the ambition of dogs. It was when he watched a man opening a can, Von Rundstedt confessed, that he felt his cultural inferiority most acutely.

It would be futile to deny that dogs are capable of mastering some aspects of human technology, at least those aspects that interest them. Every pet-lover will tell you that dogs can turn on water-faucets and drink from them. It is true that they seldom turn them off afterwards, but this is probably because they see no point in it. If a little water is wasted it is nothing to them, and besides some man will undoubtedly come along sooner or later and turn it off. There is no more technical difficulty in turning the faucet off than in turning it on, so if the dog does one and not the other it must be basically a matter of motivation. I myself have observed a Great Dane drinking from a fountain in a public park, having discovered, perhaps by accident but perhaps by a process of deduction, the foot-button that actuates the essential valve. No one could have objected to his manners; he was lapping and snapping the jet in midair without touching with any part of his mouth the orifice from which it came. In this respect his manners were better than those of many children. What I have not been able to understand so well is the extent of the dog's grasp of the principle of the water-fountain; that is, his opinion of where the water ultimately comes from, or whether he is able to distinguish in his own mind between natural and artificial sources of water. On this point I have succeeded in obtaining only contradictory and, to tell the truth, somewhat oblique opinions from dogs themselves. When, after striking up a conversation with the particular Great Dane, I suggested to him that a water-fountain was nice but after all not quite the same thing as a stream or a running brook, was it now? he fell into what seemed to me a devious kind of reticence and remarked only that water-fountains were a convenience for everyone concerned. Later I queried Von Rundstedt on this point, and as nearly as I could tell from his general comments, he could see no very great value in distinguishing between natural and artificial elements in the landscape. The pyramids of Egypt were as much a part of nature as an elm-tree; both proceeded out of natural laws and might be useful to intelligent creatures who studied their design carefully and grasped the principles of their function. I pointed out that the pyramids had actually been made by the creatures he spoke of, whereas the elm-tree had not. He then asked me what my opinion was of a coral reef. I admitted that it had been constructed by insects, but in any case they were not very intelligent creatures, and that made all the difference. Von Rundstedt ended the conversation by remarking, more to the air than to myself, that he saw very little value in this distinction.

In short, the farther I went into this relation between dogs and the human technology in which they lived, the more I encountered a tendency to reticence and deviousness in the creatures who had been so candid and even friendly when I had first taken an interest in their speech and culture. I will never forget a look that Von Runstedt and I exchanged on an occasion when I had taken him as my guest into Dorn's house. Dorn and I were in the living-room talking of something or other, and for a while I failed to notice that Von Runstedt was no longer in the room. When I finally left the room, in fact, it was not in search of him but to go to the kitchen for a drink of water. On the thick carpet my steps were soundless, and so in the kitchen I found Von Rundstedt upright with both paws on the sink. The object that interested him was screwed to the kitchen counter, and he had just discovered, my intuition told me, an important principle about it. The handle that went around and around, the most conspicuous part of its design, was not really the key or fundamental secret of its operation. You might turn the handle all you liked, but the small cutting wheel, unless you did something else, would never descend to cut what it was intended to cut. This something else was involved with an inconspicuous lever on the side of the machine that at first might have passed unnoticed. In order to carry out the operation it was necessary to raise this lever and lower it, thereby fixing the can in the machine directly under the cutting wheel and even forcing the wheel into the metal to make its initial cut, and then and only then was the time to rotate the conspicuous handle. It was really necessary to have three hands or other articulated limbs to perform this operation—one to lift the can into place, one to force down the lever and the third to begin turning the handle—and as I took in the complexity of the problem I really began to wonder how we men did it. As soon as I passed from the carpet to the linoleum and my footsteps became audible Von Rundstedt lowered himself from the counter and returned to all fours. But in the passing instant as he did so we exchanged a glance: a look profound, mocking, obscurely guilty, an expression in which were mingled a simulated innocence and an elusive but unmistable quality of complicity. On the surface this glance said nothing; it said "I put my paws on the sink to see what was up there but I was really doing nothing, and now I am wagging my tail in a doggy way to show you

I was doing nothing." But at a deeper level the glance said: we have watched you invent the spear, the campfire, the dog-catcher's truck, the gas-ovens of Auschwitz and the SPCA. Now you have invented enough. It is time for others to select among what you have invented and decide what is superfluous. As for your own superfluity, this will be obvious even to you. Henceforth if we require friends we will remember that blood is thicker than water and look for them in the Carpathians. The vigor we find there will restore our blood and recall us to our heritage. All this in a second, a half or a tenth of a second, and then Von Rundstedt was wagging his tail. I have never told Dorn about this, nor have I told anybody else.

DR. PETTIGOT'S FACE

Exactly symmetrical, with a crease in the center of the chin, it was a face that nobody would notice in a crowd except perhaps for its extraordinary blankness: it was as calm and unreadable as the visage of an antique god. One had the impression that its pale pinkish surface was capable of expression but remained for the moment immobile, perhaps through some failure of the nervous system that connected it to the mind. There was no failure of the nervous system. In fact his facial muscles were extraordinarily agile. A fly that happened to light on his brow was banished with a single twitch, and should a crumb cling to his cheek while eating it was unnecessary for him to go to the trouble of raising his napkin: a brief contraction of the Orbicular muscle, and presto! the offending morsal had fallen from sight. It was Pettigot's will that directed all these details, as it accurately did everything else in his life.

In spite of this physical reserve his outward life was normal. His digestion was excellent and he drove a four-year-old car in perfect adjustment. His clothes were conservative to the point of bizarre: knitted ties, suits with pleats in the trousers, wide-brimmed fedoras, and overshoes if there was any danger of rain. His wife Gilda, who was a good deal younger than he was (in his days as a professor of medicine he had married a student), had learned to organize the routine of the household perfectly; otherwise she was subject to his disapproval. She was an excellent cook—they both preferred health food and lived largely on cereals and vegetables—and was able to type his manuscripts, a duty that was not onerous since on the average he produced a small article only once every three or four years. Her chronic frigidity had been treated by specialists but to very little avail. For the rest she had her own life. Having given up her medical career to marry, she was free to do exactly as she pleased. Or so it seemed to Pettigot. Whose given name, known only to his wife, was Ambro, although she herself called him Kink, and so he signed the memos he left for her on the bulletin board in the kitchen. How this nickname had originated they had both forgotten.

At the Institute for Physioanalytic Study he was not very much respected by his colleagues. Working in isolation and with limited means, ignored by the scientific world at large, he was content to be regarded as a harmless eccentric. His perennial quarrels with the Director Dr. Felix Mandel over matters of budget were legendary. He himself would have been hard put to explain what his research consisted of. Although he was trained as an anatomist, his interest had turned gradually over the years to the study of behavior. But by no means did he confine himself to the physical. His real subject was the enigma that had baffled the greatest of intellects from the dawn of thought to the present: the relation between body and soul. Somewhere deep inside him man thought and felt. Outwardly he moved, his muscles twitched. What was the mechanism that connected the two? How could thought move matter; how could matter produce thought? For spirit existed in one realm, flesh entirely in another. For twenty years Pettigot cut apart cadavers, and learned: nothing. He didn't find the soul. He hadn't expected to.

He was objective, he did not prejudge the facts, and he did not allow free rein, or any rein at all, to his emotions. One of the conclusions of his twenty years of work was the fairly obvious one that the face is the chief window of the soul, and this led him to concentrate thereafter on this limited portion of the human exterior. He became an expert on the anatomy of facial expression. Assiduously he reviewed the literature, beginning with the *Physiognomy* of that odd Swiss parson Lavater (1781) and continuing through Corman and Rousseau (1882), Einbilder (1924; 1928), and Kawamoto (1940) to Bagration's definitive study *Jeux Musculaires et Expressions du Visage* (Paris, 1949). At first he was afraid that Bagration had anticipated him and the work he planned had already been done. But Bagration confined himself to the surface of the body and showed no talent, or inclination, for more profound investigations. Pettigot went on from where Bagration left off. Man, he reflected, was the only animal capable of facial expression (he rejected the claims of dog-lovers, persons who believed their canaries could show grief, and so on), and therefore the only animal whose soul could be investigated through examining his external musculature. It was well known that when a person smiled he was happy, and when he frowned, or his mouth turned down, he was sad. But this rough-cut empiricism was lacking in quantified taxonometric parameters; that is, it was too crude. There were on the human face twenty-nine separate muscles, and since they were symmetric the total was double this figure. Each could be contracted separately, or they could join together in various combinations. The total number of permutations was formidable; it ran into the hundreds of billions. But if all possible expressions could be classified—if a table or chart could be devised showing the exact equivalence in the soul of every combination of contractions—the psychologist would possess an exact instrument on which he might read the state of the organ he dealt with, just as the cardiac specialist reads the ailment of the heart in the contortions of a pen-line on paper.

Pettigot set to work with vigor and perseverance. The subject was a complex one, involving as it did anatomy, physiology, psychology, and for all one knew even metaphysics (he was not sure what he would find if he ever succeeded in reading the human soul as the cardiologist did the heart). Assiduously he haunted mental hospitals and sketched the expressions of the inmates, some of them frozen by mania into permanent grimaces. The theater too he frequented in the hope that actors, whose business it is to express emotions through the face, had accidentally stumbled on the secret he was looking for. In the lovers' lane of the city where he lived, using infra-red equipment, he painstakingly photographed the visages of ecstasy. In the laboratory he gave chocolates to little children borrowed from a nearby progressive kindergarten, on the other hand subjected them to mild electric shocks, and recorded the results in a notebook. The results were predictable: they smiled when eating chocolates, wrinkled up and burst into tears when shocked.

The problem that still thwarted him was a methodological one: how could he verify the true condition of the souls involved? How could he be sure that the little children were really enjoying the chocolates, and disenjoying the shocks—how could he be sure, for example that they didn't merely *understand that it was expected of them* to smile when given candy and cry when mistreated? He was confronted with the problem of solipsism that had baffled every other investigator from the time of the Greeks. How was it possible to know what was happening in the soul of another? And, this information lacking, how could one possibly discover the connection between body and soul? On this subject all the authorities, from Aristotle to Lavater and Bagration, were as ludicrously incompetent as himself.

The thing is, it shouldn't be imagined that because Pettigot was a highly trained and highly specialized scientist he was insensitive to the values of the humanities. He had an interest in history and collected books on the Spanish Inquisition, and he knew a good deal about Bach. At the ballet he noted with interest the conventional displacements of the limbs intended as equivalents to the passions. In literature he preferred the romantics and symbolists of the nineteenth century. Not only were these things restoring to mind and body, but occasionally they stimulated his research in unexpected ways. It was while reading "The Purloined Letter," in fact, that he discovered the crucial text of his career, the words around which his subsequent life turned as about a well-oiled pivot.

"When I wish to find out how wise, or how stupid or good, or how wicked is any one, or what are his thoughts at the moment, I fashion the expression of my face, as accurately as possible, in accordance with the expression of his, and then wait to see what thoughts or sentiments arise in my mind or heart, as if to match or correspond with the expression."

Pettigot was electrified and put down the story without finishing it. Putting Poe's theory to the test, he found that it worked. The connection between emotion and facial expression could be reversed. To smile was to produce inwardly the feeling of having something to smile about; to grimace in terror was to know a kind of terror. From that day forth he abandoned all the expensive equipment in his laboratory—the scalpels and dissecting-tables, the infra-red cameras and generators of electric shocks—in favor of a simple device obtainable in any hardware store: a mirror.

At this point he began making rapid and even dizzying progress in the research that had faltered for so many years. With the mirror installed in the center of the otherwise empty laboratory he pursued a methodology as simple as Columbus' egg, so simple it could only be a product of genius.

1. He employed only introspection; i.e., he did not have recourse to subjects other than himself.

2. In position before the mirror he contracted each of the twenty-nine facial muscles separately, and observed what mental state was thereby produced in him.

3. He deduced that inversely the existence of each of these mental states produced the contraction of the corresponding muscle or muscles.

In this early stage of work he confined himself to simple states of mind produced by the contraction of a single pair of muscles. The Frontals, for example, drew the scalp back and produced an effect of surprise. The contraction of the Zygomatics, which drew the mouth upward, gave a pleasurable sensation, while wrinkling the brow with the Corrugator supercilii threw him into deep thought. The extrinsic oculars responsible for eyeball movement (superior Rectus, inferior Rectus) controlled the position of the mind in time: to look out horizontally was to think of the present, to deflect the iris downward was to recall the past, to look upward was to contemplate the future. He took copious notes. In only a few weeks he had charted the primary emotions corresponding to each of the twenty-nine symmetrical muscles of the face.

He then moved on to complex states of mind produced

by the tension or equilibrium of two or more pairs of muscles in contraction. For example, skepticism or irony was indicated by the play of four different sets of muscles. The Zygomatics drew the mouth upward while simultaneously the Triangulars held it downward; the Buccinators and Risorius joined in a tension producing a light wrinkle in the cheek just beyond the mouth. The expression said, "Privately I am amused, but I control my amusement. Only the perceptive have noticed that what is being said, or what I am saying, has two meanings." Such combinations were intricate in their possibilities, infinite in fact. Yet, with the vast reservoir of his own emotions now available to him, the cataloguing of these relationships was only a matter of assiduous and patient effort.

It interested him greatly, so much so that his wife Gilda, coming to the laboratory one evening to find out why he had not come home to dinner, found him seated before the mirror with a notebook on his knee, making one complex expression after another.

"Ah, I'm glad you've come. What time is it anyhow? The interplay of the various platysmata surrounding the mouth is quite interesting. The Levator labii superioris, of course, is the chief elevator of the upper lip. The Levator labii superioris alaeque nasi—here—assists it and also dilates the nostrils, and together with the former and the Zygomaticus minor forms the nasolabial furrow which is deepened in expressions of sadness. When I contract all three together—as you see—I produce in myself an emotion of contempt or disdain."

She took him home; he went off willingly even though still somewhat abstracted. But the preoccupation was expanding to fill his whole life, even at the dinner table. When they had reached the stage of the salad she looked up to find him in an expression that might be described, perhaps, as Indignation Combined with Profound Moral Condemnation.

"Are you thinking of something?"

"No, I'm working."

"Without a mirror?"

Still holding the expression on his face, he suggested, "Perhaps you can serve instead. Is it true that the expression I am indicating is produced by the Frontals working in conjunction with the Corrugator supercilii to draw the skin of the brow to the center and at the same time upward? Because that corresponds to my subjective impression."

Instead of answering she posed another question. "Why is your expression indicating Indignation Combined with Profound Moral Condemnation, if you are not feeling this? Because you know, Kink, to go about making faces that have no meaning is to lose touch with reality."

"I am feeling it. What you asked me was what I am thinking of, and I am not thinking of anything. Instead the state of mind is evoked by the muscular configuration itself. Even you should be able to grasp this simple distinction." Satisfied with the results of his analysis, he abruptly relaxed his face. They proceeded to the tapioca pudding.

With the rapidity of bursting fireworks Pettigot made more discoveries, about the relation between facial expression and character, for example. For character might be defined as a state of mind prolonged to the point where it becomes permanent. A baby or young child asleep, as everyone knows, is without expression. But in older persons the years of domination by a single state of mind (avarice, timidity, disapproval) produce a permanent deformation of the face; the skin wrinkles and stretches to accommodate the soul beneath. After forty each human being wears his destiny stamped on his visage. And so Pettigot, looking at a person opposite on a bus, or a criminal between two detectives, or a face fixed momentarily in the glow of the footlights, knew for a certainty, "This is how it feels to be a prudish old maid, a child-murderer, an actress pretending to be Camille."

The actress, of course, was not a phthisic French demimondaine, only pretending to be. And this matter of simulation or mimicry injected another and unexpected complexity into his studies. The face of an actress was a trick of surfaces, a palimpsest of deception and reality. The Zygomatics and the Mentalis might indicate an expression of amorosity, for instance, while at the same time the Pretarsals and Risorius conveyed another expression that might be described as "look at me and admire, I am portraying amorosity." What under such circumstances did the actress truly feel? Pettigot, seated before his mirror, arranged his own face according to this complex state, and *knew*. Through muscular manipulation he had created in his soul an emotion previously impossible for it, that of the actress playing Camille. He had *become* an actress playing Camille. Since states of being are simply states of consciousness, he could make himself into whatever he wanted to be. There in the silence of his laboratory, empty now except for the mirror, he felt almost within his grasp the secret of human happiness, of man's final triumph over his own imperfection, and the imperfection of the world that surrounded him.

Not only his happiness, of course, but the happiness of others as well (He was not an altruist, only a rigorously objective logician.) Reflecting on his domestic environment, he turned his mind to his wife Gilda with a new and fertile surmise. That evening during a light supper of mushroom cutlets, he shared with her the subject that pressed in his mind.

"My dear, I have something to say to you."

Sensing the importance of the moment, she laid down her fork.

"Certain findings in the laboratory have suggested the possibility that your conjugal shortcomings . . ."

"My what?"

"You know very well of what I speak. It is possible, I say, that these conjugal difficulties or inadequacies might be surmounted if you could assume the proper facial expression at the appropriate time. The true feeling will come after."

She examined him, it seemed, in a new way, with a kind of curiosity. After a pause she said quietly, "The facial expression?"

"Yes."

"And what is it?"

But here Pettigot realized that he was the prisoner of his own introspective method. Having no first-hand knowledge as to what might be the facial expression accompanying female orgasm, he was unable to tell her what combination of muscles to contract so as to achieve this effect—an effect he was certain lay within her grasp if only this combination (and the term was fitting; it was a secret almost like the combination of a safe) could be determined. Assailed by a tweak of mild nostalgia, Pettigot remembered his courtship and marriage, the bright promise of those days when happiness seemed to lie like a shining garden of delights before him—before them, he corrected—the individual blossoms of which waited only to be plucked. Pettigot mused; his glance fell to the floor. (Depression of the iris below the horizontal plane; thoughts of the past.) Then it fixed on the wall opposite, and on the cornice where it joined the ceiling. (Iris in the horizontal plane, or above it; thoughts of the present and future.) Was it possible that all his years of work would fall victim to this paradox of solipsism—that he had discovered a universal system that was confined within himself, and applicable only to himself? That would indeed be an irony. Then his glance, turning to the side (lateral deflection of the iris; transition from one idea to another), moved from object to object in this familiar parlor where his domestic drama had unrolled for twenty years.

And with the brightness of epiphany the final truth struck him: happiness came not outwardly from these petty objects, these souvenir bud-vases and embroidered pillows from Atlantic City, but *inwardly from within himself.* Quite calm now, he got into his well-adjusted car and drove to the Institute. It was eleven o'clock at night, and a Sunday at that, but he had a key. Quickly admitting himself to his laboratory, he switched on the light and took up his place before the mirror. The expression he had to assume now was a complex one: "The eminent behavioral researcher taking satisfaction in the fact that, after years of misunderstanding and neglect, his ideas are accepted by the scientific community, so that at last he basks in a well-merited celebrity and acclaim." After a number of false starts he found the right combination of muscles to contract. The major and minor Zygomatics were drawn into especially powerful play, forming a smile which was modified by the Frontals raising the brow in mild and modest deprecation. The four Auricular muscles were in tension, while the Levators and Risorius held the mouth in a configuration of light contempt. The Buccinators were firm, flattening the cheeks in satisfaction. And with this last adjustment, as though a searching hand had unexpectedly found the combination of a safe, the sensation of happiness came. His faith in himself was justified. He had arrived at the goal of his years of patient work.

Behind him, entering the laboratory softly, came the others to share in his triumph: his beloved wife Gilda, the Director of the Institute, Dr. Mandel, who had so often been his enemy in the past, and a pair of young men in white scientific garb who had no doubt come to add their kudos to the general esteem.

Gilda seemed to be in a most considerate, even affectionate humor. Softly, with the air of revealing the details of a pleasant surprise, she informed him that there were to be some changes in the living arrangements. She, at least for the present, would go on living in the house. For him a spacious room had been reserved at the Greenbrook Academy for Persons of Exceptional Mentality. It was great good fortune and an honor that the Academy had agreed to accept him. Not everyone (and Dr. Mandel at her elbow agreed!) had the necessary qualifications for a Fellowship. And these young men (they were then, as he had surmised, minor representatives of the scientific community) had come to accompany him there and see to it that his every want and comfort was provided for.

Now, it shouldn't be imagined that Pettigot was taken in by his wife's suave words. He knew very well what kind of a place the Academy was. But he knew also something that they didn't know and nobody knew but himself, that none of it mattered. He would be happy there and happy anywhere, if he were allowed to take his mirror. He was allowed to take his mirror. One of the young men carried it for him. The other deferentially guided him at his elbow.

And behold Pettigot. It has come to pass exactly as he foresaw and planned. At the Academy, in a large clean room filled with sunlight, he grimaces incessantly, in a banquet, an orgy, of satisfaction. He knows esteem, praise, the warmth of long labor rewarded, the envy of lesser rivals. The greater and lesser Zygomatics, through constant smiling, have become noticeably larger in size. He spends his waking hours at the mirror and goes to bed content. Is he mad? The question of who is mad and who is not is a fine one. Dr. Pettigot is doing all right. He has his own opinion of your life, just as you have your opinion of his.

AFTERWORD

Surely the most dismal science is not economics but autocriticism. *Apologia pro opera sua.* What can I say about my own work? Invent anecdotes, tell lies, pat the stunted child on the head along with the others, bask in the warmth of explaining in detail my specialness to a captive audience. Will you get a chance to explain how clever *you* are? No, because this is not a cocktail party, and they don't have books that work two ways yet. But perhaps you would like to know something about how these artful fictions came into being.

I have looked up *opera*, by the way, and it can be a singular feminine noun. I don't know a scrap about Latin. I clearly remember the circumstance under which I wrote "Dr. Pettigot's Face." I was in Paris and rather bored from having been there too long—what an effete person, bored in Paris!—and I was idly looking through some bookstalls in the Latin Quarter, near the School of Medicine, when I came across a book called *Jeux Musculaires et Expressions du Visage*, by Docteur Roger Ermiane. It seemed to me a mad book then and it still does. I was fascinated by the drawings, which were crude and evidently drawn by the author, and which tended to induce madness in the reader if stared at too long. I took the book home and resolved to write a story about it. It seemed to me it would be very little work; Dr. Ermiane was already quite mad enough to be a character in a fiction. As a matter of fact, I had to spend several tedious afternoons in the American Library, trying with only partial success to find the English translations for the names of the fifty-eight separate muscles of the human face. The story wrote itself; I only had to add a wife, and an ending.

"Dr. Pettigot's Face" was published in *The Iowa Review*, then several years later something I read in the newspaper caught my attention. It was probably some kind of a hoax, but anyhow I sent an offprint of the story to a researcher named Paul Ekman on the faculty of the University of California, San Francisco. Not only was Professor Ekman a perfectly respectable scientist, but it turned out that he was aware of the earlier work of Dr. Ermiane, and moreover that he had gone past the point where Ermiane had stopped, and on to the discovery that I myself had fancied: that, once the expressions corresponding to various emotions are known, we can induce those emotions by fixing our faces into those expressions. As one of Professor Ekman's papers put it, "moving the face voluntarily changes physiology."

I make no claim, as Borges does, that the inventing of fictions can bring into the world real objects that have been charmed into existence by the power of the fiction itself. I simply think it is curious that science was in this way paralleled by art, and art constructed by a person who does not understand even one iota of science and has a basically unscientific mind. But I will make the claim that fiction can be an act of discovery, that it can disclose states of mind, or soul, that were previously invisible and in fact *did not exist* until fiction offered a husk in which they could take shape in our consciousness. Before Proust we could not have Proustian experiences; before Kafka our modern bureaucracies could not be Kafkaesque as they have since become. Let us now all close our eyes and try to induce happiness by screwing up our faces into smiles.

However I see I am not explaining these stories in the right order. Several years ago I set out foolishly to write an epic of Marco Polo's voyage in modern dress, but was beaten to it by Gary Jennings, who came out with his own book *The Journeyer*, so much better researched than mine, and so much more stupendous and pornographic. I moved among my own wreck salvaging the better parts, and came out first with the novella "Polo's Trip" which begins this book. I took a delight in writing parts of it and hope you catch the more obscure jokes (Col Ducon is obscene in French, and Koni means the same thing in Sanscrit). I wish I could think of something else for Gresseth to do, he is too good to throw away on a novella, and Lieutenant Mu at the border is an underemployed character too. The camel Sylvia in this tale is another one of my characters of whom I am genuinely fond, which illustrates the bewitching power of fiction because I am sure I could not love any camel in real life. This novella will give you a useful and practical set of instructions for skinning a ram.

"The Linguist" and "The Martyred Poet" are more dismembered parts of this same Polo project, the Cathay Stories of my present title. Whether there could be three sexes, or whether anyone will ever devise such a complicated execution machine, only time will tell. Perhaps there will be three sexes as soon as we invent terms for them, and for the complicated acts that result from their existence. As for "The Martyred Poet," can we not believe that the doctors are clever enough, or will become clever enough in the future, to make a severed head speak?

"Little Eddy" is not a dismembered part, but it is a longish story, or a shortish novella, that started off as a novel and rounded itself off to exactly this length. Some people find it obscure and say there are too many literary references in it. I think there are just the right number of literary references, but I do find the story obscene and a little disturbing, in spite of its efforts to be funny. This is a story with its pants down, and the results are somewhat amusing but also not pleasant to look at, so let us pull the pants up again quickly. If I didn't go on with Popo, it is because the things that happen to him later are even more unpleasant.

I find Venice as a city both morbid and ludicrous. I also love it very much. And then I love bassoons, they are my favorite instruments in the orchestra, with their honking tones and their clownish efforts to be dignified. The joke at the bottom of "The Orphan Bassoonist" is an old one, the little boy who killed his parents so he could go to the Orphans' Picnic. There are only a certain number of stories in the human collective unconscious, and this anecdote, with its travelogue bits, is a loving effort to induce life into a durable old mummy. My impulse for writing the story was not quite this, however; it was the thought that if Vivaldi really existed, and really forced little girls in an orphanage to master his concerti, he must have been a sadist.

"The Photograph" I wrote in Paris, about the same time as "Dr. Pettigot's Face." Do you hear the song in the back of my head? Is it in the back of your head too, or are you too young? "I'm gonna sit right down and write myself a letter, and make believe it came from you." Please do not read any undertones of homosexuality, or undertones of anything else, into this extended joke which ends well enough, since it is almost impossible to shoot yourself under the belief that you are shooting somebody else. A certain son of mine, who was about ten at the time, said, "What a jerk." And I couldn't agree more.

If there is a stunted child here, hiding behind its mother's skirts, it is "The Fun Dome." God knows how I wrote it. I must have been smoking something, and not very good quality either. Caspian is one of a number of blushers, goofers, and inept persons in my fiction, an alter ego perhaps, or a half of one; I can hope that my other half is more like Proctor. And yet, who at one time or another has not longed to pick up a girl named Bonnie in a Fun Zone? And what would happen if you did? Fun, perhaps, although more likely it would turn out as it does in this story. So the reader is forewarned. This is a moral tale for young men, one that admonishes you not to frequent bad companions and get into the kind of trouble that Caspian gets into. Does anyone detect French surrealism in this story? I tried as well as I could to conceal it, although the tram is perhaps a dead giveaway for Paul Delvaux.

The question of just what is going on inside animals is one that has always mesmerized me. We can't help anthropomorphizing them, and this prevents us from understanding anything at all about them. These helpless objects of our affection and libido, these entertaining cartoon puppets, these actors wearing dog skins and lions' manes, are entirely in our minds. But they are vastly interesting, and they do seem to suggest to us numbers of profound things that we can't really lay our fingers on. How does it feel to be a giraffe, or a ferret? For a fiction writer, these cousin existences are only forms of characterization. So the dogs of "The Dog Mafia" are not real dogs, but only ourselves wrapped in amusing pelts and skins, and telling us home truths we won't admit to ourselves. I know that a dog can work a water fountain, and I believe that in time some dog may learn how to use a can opener. But that is not the point. The narrator in this story is of course mentally ill (I see now that so many of my characters are mad! What can be the significance of that?) and the dogs that speak to him are inside himself, telling him things that otherwise might remain hidden forever in his occiput. He knows a little about linguistics and can talk in an interesting way about it; it's too bad about his illness, otherwise he might have become a professor, or a teacher of creative writing.

BIO NOTE

MacDonald Harris is the author of thirteen novels, including *The Balloonist*, *Herma*, *Screenplay*, and *Glowstone*. His short fiction has appeared in magazines ranging from *The Atlantic Monthly* and *Harper's* to *Esquire*, *The Iowa Review*, and *Prairie Schooner*. He is on the staff of the Writing Program at the University of California, Irvine.